D1624801

THE (Desperate) DIVA DIARIES

CATIE CONRAD:
Faith, Friendship, and Fashion Disasters!

Chic!

ANGIE SPADY

with Channing Everidge

B&H PUBLISHING GROUP
Nashville, Tennessee

To: Ariel
[signature] Spady

DEDICATION

To Mom:
For teaching me that fashions are fun
but being a woman of faith
is even more fabulous.

FRIDAY, MARCH 12

Okay, so why does ANYONE try shopping for me??? ESPECIALLY MY PARENTS!

I happen to have EXCELLENT taste and know EXACTLY what I do and do not need!

THIS JOURNAL FALLS INTO THE I-DO-NOT-NEED CATEGORY.

It's all Dad's fault.

"Here are those sketchbooks you asked me to pick up, Catie. And for just $9.99, you get two for the price of one!"

THESE ARE NOT SKETCHBOOKS! THEY'RE DIARIES!

NOT!

NOT!

NOT!

CATIE CONRAD'S RIDICULOUS DIARIES ☹

WHAT WAS DAD THINKING??

I'm surprised that he didn't buy some kind of zit zapper on top of everything else. At least THAT I could actually use!

The goop that Mom bought me doesn't even faze my worst pimple— which happens to be the size of a small state. ☹ There's not enough goop on the planet to cover the small volcano growing on my chin. I thought about wearing a ski mask to school, but Mom said I'm the only one who even notices the "tiny bump." Yeah, right!

Me and the rest of the human population!!!

Just because Dad works for a magazine and likes to write about boring stuff doesn't mean I want to! **UGH!** ☹

NOT. NOT. NOT.

Surely Dad knows I plan on being the next FASHIONISTA EXTRAORDINAIRE—**"THE FAMOUS CATIE CONRAD"**—which is what they'll print in *Ooh La La* magazine. I don't plan on wasting my time writing in a diary.

Instead of writing like Dad, I'll be designing the latest and greatest fashions for New York and Rome . . . even PARIS!

And I won't just be sketching ideas, I'll bring them to life. That is, IF Mom's old sewing machine cooperates. She even lets me keep it in my room since I never know when a brilliant idea might pop into my head.

I'm working on the coolest hand-bag EVER. I read that tons of the famous designers got started that way. All it took was a quick trip to Goodwill, ten old ties, and TA-DA: The "Totally Tie Bag!" Who knows, it could be the next big thing, and I'll be known all over the state . . . or maybe even the world!

I do NOT have time to write in a diary. Do I have time to sketch and create gorgeous fashions? Yes. Write about boring ol' stuff? No.

I'm positive Sophie will agree this diary is the most ridiculous thing ever.

Sophie Martin is my best friend, and she always gives me great advice. Whether it's about which way my hair looks best (Sophie's hair is naturally curly and ALWAYS looks amazing) or if I need to calm down over the latest drama at school, Sophie's always there for me. We're even in the same Sunday school class at church. That girl can memorize verses like it's the easiest thing in the world. (I'm glad someone can!)

AND, I might add, Sophie LOVES my fashion designs. She's sort of like my very own fashion critic—who has excellent taste, of course. ☺

At least now I have plenty of sketch paper, er, I mean diary paper, for my drawings. If I'm really lucky, maybe one of my designs will end up on the runway in Paris, and I'll have Dad to thank for that. ☺

Maybe I'll write just a little in this diary—IF I get time. Dad was super excited to give it to me, after all. I eked out a small, "Gee, thanks, Dad" and tried to be nice. If I didn't, I'd get chewed out by Mom, and she'd say, "When are you going to start appreciating things, young lady?" Then I'd get the I'm-sooo-disappointed-in-you look and everything would go downhill from there.

Mom's right, even though I don't like admitting it. I guess I need to be a little more thankful. Okay, okay . . . A LOT more thankful. I'm pretty blessed to have a Dad who cares for me, not to mention having a Father in heaven who loves me too! I know Sophie would agree with me 1,000 percent.

But I will NOT be a reporter like Dad. Every single night he's up late on his computer. One minute he's on the phone, then back to the computer, and on and on and on. And he says I'M on the computer too much?

SHEESH!

Dad writes "human interest" stories—whatever that means. I guess it's about stuff humans are supposed to be interested in, but not me. I never read those grown-up magazines. The stuff is kind of interesting though . . . sometimes. Once he wrote about a group of missionaries in Haiti who needed art supplies for summer camp. **STRANGE**. I could NOT imagine a life without art supplies!

So we all pitched in and did a fund-raiser for the school. I even cleared out my craft boxes in my closet and sent that stuff too. A few months later, the students sent us some cool drawings using the art materials we'd mailed.

Mom still has one of the drawings on the refrigerator, along with a few of my fashion sketches.

Hmmm . . . maybe I'll keep my Prayer List in my diary?? That's a thought. Mom says it helps her remember to pray for all sorts of things—like the kids in Haiti.

PRAYER LIST

1. Pray for the kids in Haiti and that God supplies them with their needs.

2. Pray that Dad understands I don't like writing as much as he does!

SATURDAY, MARCH 13

SPA SLEEPOVER!!!! YES!

So Sophie and I decided to try and come up with a new zit eraser formula last night. I'm sure it was attempt #137 or something like that. There just HAS to be something that smells better than the gross store stuff. We also read online that cotton balls soaked in vinegar and lemon juice would make our skin sparkle. We even put cucumber slices on our eyes to get an extra boost. BIG MISTAKE. The only thing that happened is we ended up smelling like a PICKLE FACTORY. We even had to sleep with the windows open in my room.

My eight-year-old brother, Jeremy (I prefer to call him "the GERM"), went around the house with a clothespin on his nose, yelling "PEE-YEW! GIRLS STINK!"

WHAT A BRAT!

He even put a clothespin on the nose of his pet skunk, Rosey. Yes, he has a skunk for a pet! Can you say **WEIRD**? But why would a skunk need a clothespin on her nose, when "Stink" is her middle name!!

Why???

(Note: I would need an ENTIRE diary to tell you about my brat of a brother. . . . There's probably not enough paper in the world to explain him!)

Actually, spa disasters seem to follow me wherever I go. Last week, when I was at Sophie's house, we read online that a milk and oatmeal bubble bath was the "ultimate spa ritual." We put on our swimsuits, filled the bathtub with warm water and milk and added a whole box of oatmeal.

EPIC FAIL.

Not only did it NOT work, but we were also a STICKY MESS. I'm not sure which was the most embarrassing: being in a bathtub wearing my swimsuit or having oatmeal stuck to my scalp. Sophie's parents got totally mad (Mr. Martin is the school PRINCIPAL, I might add), and there was no milk left for cereal the next morning.

NEVER AGAIN.
I REPEAT: NEVER AGAIN!

But Sophie CAN dream up the most SCRUMPTIOUS body scrubs! From coconut to strawberry to chocolate, she can mix up some delish stuff to slather on our arms and legs. I'm always tempted to reach down and lick my arms, but then that would be acting like a first grader.

Sophie will definitely be a scientist, or maybe a world-famous chef someday. She makes the most DELISH brownies ever—chocolate chunk peanut butter—that will MELT in your mouth. She doesn't even have to use a measuring cup because she says she has the recipe MEMORIZED. It's no wonder she's the brainiac in science class. She remembers science definitions as quickly as she does those Bible verses.

Why didn't I get that gift? I forget EVERYTHING! In fact, I'm trying to memorize this Bible verse so I can have more patience with the Germ.

JAMES 1:12
GOD BLESSES THOSE WHO PATIENTLY ENDURE TESTING AND TEMPTATION. AFTERWARD THEY WILL RECEIVE THE CROWN OF LIFE THAT GOD HAS PROMISED TO THOSE WHO LOVE HIM.

PRAYER LIST
Add #3, "Patience with the Germ," to my Prayer List!

SUNDAY, MARCH 14

I am SOOOO being tested today! The Germ is driving me **INSANE**. Mom goes on and on and on and on about me needing to develop "a little more patience" with my baby brother. EASY FOR HER TO SAY.

I even asked Sophie to pray that I could tolerate the Germ a little more. She and I are in the same Sunday school class, and I needed all the help I could get!

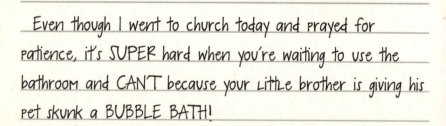

NOTE TO SELF: REMEMBER JAMES 1:12!

Even though I went to church today and prayed for patience, it's SUPER hard when you're waiting to use the bathroom and CAN'T because your little brother is giving his pet skunk a BUBBLE BATH!

ARE YOU KIDDING ME?!!!!!!!

I made Mom disinfect the entire bathroom! If I find out the Germ used my spa lotion that Sophie and I made last week, then he is DEAD MEAT. Once he got into my zit cream and covered his whole face with it! I dared him to do it again—I'd squeeze him like a real pimple, and THEN he'd be sorry! Why do I have to be the one with the crazy brother who likes girly lotion?

WHY????????????

I've decided to just hang out in my room and stay here as long as possible. Of course, I'll have to come out and eat . . . AND use the bathroom. ☹ ☹ ☹ Maybe the stink will disappear while I draw in my sketchbook.

I get all of my inspiration from Claire Hunter, who is THE coolest young designer on Earth. I subscribe to her blog and keep up with all of her latest stuff online. They even sell a few of her things at Unique Boutique at the Clairemont Ridge mall. Which is exactly why I'm trying to save my money and buy something from her spring collection. ☺

I've also got the most AMAZING idea for a skirt that I just have to get out on paper. I'm actually going to "redo" one of Mom's old skirts and bring it into the 21st century. With just a little bling, a hot glue gun, and a few tucks here and there, I MIGHT even wear it to school one of these days if I get the nerve.

If only I could be famous like Claire Hunter and all those other designers. That would be sooo cool! Then I'd be rich! THEN I could build my OWN bathroom and BAN THE GERM FOR LIFE!

Oh, and I just wouldn't have my own bathroom, I'd have my **VERY OWN DESIGN STUDIO!** That would be the greatest thing EVER!

The 5 *MUSTS* for a Catie Conrad Design Studio

1. Mannequins everywhere, wearing my designs, of course. ☺

2. Sewing machines—at least three. (You never know when one might break down!)

3. Fabrics from all over the world (sequined, shiny, plaid, neon—you get the idea). ☺

4. A refrigerator full of my favorite foods—and a microwave, of course. (A designer has to eat!)

5. Candles that smell like birthday cakes. Or maybe strawberries? Or sugar cookies?

ANYTHING BUT GERM SCENT!!!

Just thinking about the GERM and Rosey puts me in a bad mood all over again. I cannot WAIT to vent to Sophie at school tomorrow. And show her my new skirt design. The sooner the better!!!!!!

NOTE TO SELF: Read James 1:12—AGAIN!!!

MONDAY, MARCH 15

Did I say I wanted to see Sophie at school?
SCRATCH THAT THOUGHT! ☹

But I'LL admit it's because I'M TOTALLY jealous, which I
know is not the right way to be. **NOTE TO SELF:
ADD "DON'T BE JEALOUS OF OTHER
PEOPLE'S STUFF" TO MY PRAYER LIST!**

This morning Sophie
waltzed into first period
class with a new CELL
PHONE! Yes, that's what I
said, a BEAUTIFUL,
AMAZING, HIGH-TECH
smartphone with TEXT,
INTERNET, ITUNES, ETC.,
ETC.!!!

The Most
Amazing
Phone
EVER!

She even has a cool case with a pink cupcake on the back.
Not only do I want a phone like hers sooo bad, but it looks
good enough to eat!

Of course she could have texted me last night to prepare me for this surprise, but she couldn't. WHY? **BECAUSE I DON'T HAVE A CELL PHONE THAT TEXTS!**

I found out later that Sophie's been doing extra chores at home to earn money to buy it, but that STILL didn't make me feel any better. . . .

So now the two girls in my class with the coolest cell phones are my best friend AND the school snob:

MIRANDA MARONI.

At least Sophie can't stand Miranda either.

Miranda thinks she is IT and always has the latest and greatest of everything. And the WORST thing about it is, she rubs it in our faces. If a cool bag is in *Teen Vogue* magazine (which she carries around like it's her Bible!), she has it before anyone else. She'll even "accidentally" drop the magazine on the floor and say, "Oh, that is so cool. But I forgot, I already have it."

.UGH.

If there are some great boots in the Shoe Plus store window, then Miranda has the first pair and struts around in them at school. One day she hiked her big foot up onto Sophie's desk, just to make sure we saw her new sequined sneakers. **WHO CARES!!!!!!!!!!!!**

Oh, and Miranda's cell phone has **bling, bling, bling,** WITH an amazing zebra case, I might add. That phone has more ring tones than Apple! And she's always on it at break, playing some game when she isn't supposed to.

Just once, I wish she'd get busted by Mrs. Gibson. (Note to self: pray about not wishing the worst on Miranda Maroni.)

But it's sooooo hard. She even tried to kiss up to Sophie in class this morning.

Miranda: "Sophie, your phone is soooo cool! It's ALMOST as cool as mine! You need to come over to my house, and maybe we can shop for some new ring tones or cases. You can even bring over some of those weird cookies you make!"

BLAH BLAH BLAH!!!!

Just because Miranda's dad works at a bank, she thinks she can have ANYTHING and EVERYTHING she wants. But I can't.

My parents have normal jobs, and that's okay by me . . . most of the time. Mom even takes coupons to the grocery, and we TRY to stay within our budget as much as possible. Sometimes it's even fun to try and see how much money we can save up for vacation and stuff. Dad also reminds us to tithe at church. Sometimes it feels like a total bummer after I've worked so hard for my allowance and then have to turn around and give it away.

I've tried to explain to him that I'm saving up for a Claire Hunter brand outfit. Of course I can ALWAYS use new fabric for my next design too. But I know it's important to obey God's commands—even if it is hard.

Speaking of hard, it's SUPER hard not to tell Miranda what I really think. Of course I want to explode into a zillion pieces, but I TRY not to let those thoughts come out of my mouth.

5...4...3...2...1

One minute I almost think Miranda could be nice if she tried, but the next minute she's making fun of my hair, my clothes, or whatever else she can make fun of. Sophie's too.
WHAT DID WE EVER DO TO HER?

And Emily Wheeler has been her sidekick ever since fourth grade. Emily can sometimes act friendly, but whenever Miranda is around, she's just as rude. **STRANGE.** WHY Emily puts up with Miranda I have NO IDEA! Maybe it's because they're both on the volleyball team or something. Of course Miranda is not only the most popular girl at school, she's also the best volleyball player around. She leads the team in spikes. **UGH.**

STILL, if you ask me, that's NO REASON to be friends with Miranda. I'm surprised she doesn't make EMiLy carry her lunch tray or fetch her gym bag like her personal servant. And you know what? EMiLy would probably do it because she thinks Miranda is the center of the universe. ☹

I DO NOT GET THOSE GIRLS.

NOTE TO SELF: Add EMiLy Wheeler to my Prayer List!

TUESDAY, MARCH 16

T. T. T. **TOTALLY. TERRIBLE. TUESDAY.**

I'll probably need the rest of the week to recuperate from the news.

Why did Sophie's dad, Principal Martin, have to destroy a perfectly good Tuesday?

WHY?????? It's obvious that principals are taught how to do this in college. I'm sure Principal Martin got an A+ in "Day Wrecking 101."

"Attention All Middle School Students:

The big spring dance will be held on April 16, and I'm sure everyone is filled with excitement! I expect everyone to be on their best behavior. Boys, I expect you to act like gentleman; girls, I expect you to behave like ladies."

HUH? WHAT DID THAT EVEN MEAN??

What century did Mr. Old School live in? Ladies? Gentlemen? He was speaking a language I didn't even understand! No wonder some of the kids call him Mr. Martian instead of Mr. Martin.

I don't call him that because Sophie is my best friend. But I have to admit Mr. Martin is starting to sound a little weird! Scratch that . . . A LOT WEIRD.

Luckily, Sophie can translate her dad's Old School Alien Talk into Reality Language. I messaged her on my computer after school.

Me: OK, so I am FREAKING OUT!

Sophie: About what?

Me: Oh My Gracious! YOU KNOW—THE DANCE!

Sophie: It's gonna be awesome, don't U think?!

Me: ???? It will ONLY be awesome if "u know who" asks me to go!

Sophie: CHILL OUT. Let's go together or meet at the gym. Guess you'll just have to wait and see about "u know who."☺

Me: G2G freak out about what u just said. TTYL!!!

I CANNOT BELIEVE THIS IS HAPPENING!

Sophie's dad has TOTALLY LOST IT! I'm not sure if this is a good day or a total bummer day to be friends with Sophie. I know she can't tell her dad what to do (I CAN ONLY WISH), but the fact that he's practically forcing the guys to ask the girls to the dance is **TOTALLY INSANE!**

WHAT IF NOBODY ASKS ME TO THE DANCE?

Sometimes it's cool being best friends with the principal's kid (like when we get free leftovers at the concession stand after a ball game), BUT sometimes it can totally stink. Like the day I was super late to class because I was in the bathroom trying to fix my hair. I'd just had my bangs trimmed the night before, and I looked like a third grader. (Can you say **NIGHTMARE HAIRCUT?**) There was NO WAY I was walking into class first, in front of Miranda. I would have NEVER heard the end of it.

Mr. Martin made me write a three-page paper on "Why Being Late for Class Is Unbecoming to a Student." Sophie's dad didn't cut me any slack whatsoever! And now Mr. Martin was ruining my day—*AGAIN!*

WHAT WAS HE THINKING???

Of course, I already know who I wish would ask me to the spring dance: **JOSH HENDERSON!!!!**

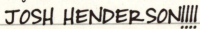

It's a no-brainer. He's the tallest and cutest guy in sixth grade. We even go to the same church! And I'm not sure if it's deodorant or cologne, but he always smells nice. Oh, and did I mention that he always prays before he eats his lunch?

I DO THE SAME THING! ☺

PERFECT!

But here's the bad part: he's pretty SHY and doesn't talk a whole LOT—especially not to ME! Maybe he'll change before the dance and ask me to go with him. After all, he could ask me at church if he wanted.

I can already picture what kind of dress I'd wear to the dance. . . .

I can only imagine what kind of dress Miranda will wear. I'm sure it will be the **LATEST AND GREATEST**, and Sophie and I will never hear the end of it!

BLAH, BLAH, BLAH, BLAH!!

WEDNESDAY, MARCH 17

Just when I thought that Tuesday was terrible,
WEDNESDAY WAS THE WORST!
The only thing on everyone's mind was THE DANCE,
THE DANCE, THE DANCE!

Some of the girls had already decided what color of dress they wanted and were making plans to go shopping together. Some were even looking at Teen Vogue or Glamour Girl and taping pics of dresses onto their lockers.
BUT THEN SOPHIE AND I OVERHEARD THE
WORST. THING. EVER.

Miranda and Emily were at their lockers and talking so loud that people on Mars could hear them.

Miranda: Oh, Emily, I am SO excited about the dance. Now . . . who do I want to go with?

Emily: This dance is going to be awesome! EVERY BOY in middle school will want to ask you to the dance, Miranda.

After all, you're the most popular girl in our class. I bet I already know who you hope will ask you, right?

Miranda: **JOSH HENDERSON!** He is by far the cutest guy in our class. I hope he'll ask me soon. Otherwise, I'll be forced to go with someone I don't even like. Or even worse—GO BY MYSELF.

Emily: I'm sure Josh will ask you. It's only a matter of time. You guys will be the cutest couple at the dance!

Miranda: Oh, thanks, Emily. Let's go dress shopping on Friday! Of course, we can always ask that crazy Catie Conrad to design a dress for us. She thinks that she's a fashion diva! **NOT. LOL!!!**

I rushed to the bathroom as quickly as possible, and Sophie wasn't far behind me.

I won't lie: I cried. ☹ ☹

Even though I was sooo angry at Miranda, I couldn't keep from crying over what she'd said about me. How could one girl be so **MEAN?!**

And JOSH HENDERSON! How could she? Miranda could get any boy in middle school to ask her to this goofy crazy insane dance. WHY DID SHE HAVE TO PICK JOSH?

THIS WAS SO NOT FAIR!

Sophie tried to make me feel better, but it was no use:

Sophie: Catie, I know it's hard, but you're going to have to ignore Miranda. What she said about you was SO WRONG. I don't know what's gotten into her. If you ask me, I think we need to pray for her. I know it seems crazy, but I think that's what we should do.

Me: Thanks Soph, but I just don't know if I can do that. She acts like a total SNOB. Why does she hate me so much? What did I ever do to her?

Sophie: You haven't done anything to her. And no matter what Miranda Maroni says, you're an AWESOME designer! But remember what we studied in Bible class a few weeks ago? In Matthew, Jesus says to love your enemies and pray for those who persecute you. And remember Joseph's own brothers threw him into a pit and then sold him! HORRIBLE!!

Sophie always knew just what to say to make me feel better.
I was so thankful she was my best friend. Being thrown in a
pit or sold off as a slave sort of made what Miranda had
said not seem so bad. When I went inside the stall to use
the bathroom, I also said a prayer for Miranda, and for God
to bless her. It was one of the hardest things I've ever done
at school, . . . but I did it anyway.

However, I STILL couldn't quit thinking about the dance.
What if everybody has a date but me? I know I can go with
Sophie, but it's not the same.

After school, I went
home and got out my
sketchbook and pencils.
Drawing and designing
makes me feel happy.
And even if Miranda
makes fun of me, I know
at least Sophie thinks my
clothes are cool.

I came up with a few decent dress designs and hung them up on my wall. I also drew some total FLOPS that wound up in the trash can. But one of them I really liked more than the others.

EVEN Miranda might like it!!

Or not . . .

WHO CARES!

THURSDAY, MARCH 18

.UGH. I could hardly wait to get home and write about the HORRIBLE thing that happened today! My day had started out so AWESOME but then suddenly took a giant **NOSE DIVE!**

Sooooo, here's what happened: Even though Miranda had made fun of me yesterday about being a fashion designer, I decided to brave it and carry my Totally Tie Bag to school. Sophie said it looked like something that even the famous designer Claire Hunter would create. Of course, Sophie is my BFF and is supposed to say things like that. The ties I used in the bag were in every shade of blue and purple. It totally matched the sweater I was wearing to school.

But to my surprise, everyone LOVED IT! Sophie repeated twice that it was the coolest bag she'd ever seen and no one could copy it in a million years. Even Emily walked past my locker and quickly said "Cool bag, Catie" before joining up with Miranda and acting as snobby as usual.

By the time I got to art class (where I totally rule), I was having one of the best days EVER! Mrs. Gibson loved my bag and said it showed "great imagination" and reflected my creative personality. Coming from an incredible art teacher like Mrs. Gibson, that means a lot! ☺

Miranda was her typical snobby self in class, but even that couldn't put me in a bad mood. I was sitting in my *favorite class* AND with my *favorite teacher*—and I was having a fantastic day.

Mrs. Gibson (BTW, did I say just how AMAZING my art teacher is?) had been teaching us about mosaics. Last week, she showed us pics of beautiful mosaic windows in churches around the world. UNBELIEVABLE. Some of them were even created to look like scenes from the Bible! How in the world artists made pictures of Jesus using tiny pieces of glass, I had NO CLUE.

AWESOME mosaic windows!

Since it was too expensive to use fancy glass, we were going to make mosaics out of tiny pieces of tile, beads, and even dried pasta. Yeah, WEIRD! Mrs. Gibson said we could even use our imagination and come up with other things to add to our project.

Our assignment was to create a mosaic of something that was special to us personally. HMMMMM . . . My mind went TOTALLY BLANK.

Mrs. Gibson showed us examples of mosaics that kids did last year, and they were INCREDIBLE to say the least. Talk about **HARD!**

I had no idea WHAT to do. I really got nervous when Mrs. Gibson gave each of us a pair of tweezers so we could pick up and glue the tiny pieces to our paper.

I needed an idea to pop into my head and FAST! Suddenly it came to me: MY SEWING MACHINE. Yes! It was definitely something I used every day, and it was also special to Mom. If my art project turned out decent, I might even give it to Mom for Mother's Day.

After four long and STRESSFUL attempts, I finally sketched a drawing of the sewing machine and outlined it with tiny black beads. My mind was already racing on what kind of other things I could bring from home to add to my mosaic. My fingers got a MAJOR CRAMP after holding those tweezers so long. ☹ Is that how Dr. Hamilton feels when he's poking around in my mouth with those awful dental tools?

After what seemed like forever, I had filled in only a TINY section of my mosaic. UGH. This would take an ETERNITY to complete. Everyone really had to be careful not to bump into one another's work because one small nudge would cause the pieces to start flying all over the place.

I shouldn't have been surprised when I saw what Miranda had chosen to create: A volleyball. I'm shocked that she wasn't doing a picture of a MIRROR.

If you ask me, Miranda's volleyball looked more like an egg, but of course no one noticed because Miranda is the Most Popular and Perfect Girl to everyone. I even over-heard Emily say, "Miranda, I think yours is soooo unique, in an artsy kind of way!"

Of COURSE Emily would say that. She's Emily—Miranda's Biggest and Only Fan. Apparently Emily also needed glasses because there was NO way Miranda's mosaic was "artsy." It was more like "flopsy" if you ask me.

But I didn't say anything. I was trying not to say the mean things that were floating around in my head.

(DID I MENTION THAT IS SOOOOO HARD?)

Even though Sophie had the best idea in the entire class, it didn't look too good. She'd decided to do a mosaic of a cross, but her lines weren't that straight. "Now you know why I don't like art!" she said, very frustrated with the whole thing.

I KNOW I heard Miranda laugh a little when she walked by Sophie's project. **HOW RUDE!**

I could tell Sophie was totally embarrassed, and I tried to make her feel better. "Hey, at least you've got the right idea, Soph. Jesus dying on the cross for us is more important than anything!" I said. "I should have thought of that too."

I made SURE to say it loudly so Miranda could hear me.

BUT THAT'S WHEN THE NOSE DIVE PART OF MY DAY HAPPENED. ☹☹☹

When Mrs. Gibson was in the back of the room grading papers, Miranda "accidentally" bumped my desk! BEADS FLEW EVERYWHERE. It sounded like popcorn kernels— flying all over the floor.

IT WAS RUINED!

All Miranda could do was bat her eyelashes and eke out an "Oops, sorry, Catie Conrad," and then cover up what I KNOW was a smile.

GRRRR . . . She did it on purpose, and everyone knew it! Everyone but Mrs. Gibson.

She tries to see the best in everyone, which is the right way to be, I GUESS. But for the life of me, I CANNOT see ANYTHING good about Miranda Maroni.

NOT ONE SINGLE THING.

ALL That hard work, DESTROYED!

I quickly tried to glue the beads again, but it was no use. The harder I tried, the worse it became—I even ended up with three fingers glued together! It was a DISASTER.

And since we only have art once a week (which is SO not fair), I'll probably get a nice fat **F** for **FLOP** on this project. I'll be embarrassed for life because everyone knows I am . . . or *WAS* the best artist in class.

WELL, NOT ANYMORE. ☹ ☹

THANKS FOR NOTHING, MIRANDA MARONI.

Add to Prayer List: Act like Mrs. Gibson and TRY to find SOMETHING nice about Miranda, even though

(A) she ruined my art project and

(B) she is SO RUDE to me!

FRIDAY, MARCH 19

I'VE NEVER BEEN SO GLAD TO SEE FRIDAY IN MY ENTIRE LIFE!

I thought Miranda might apologize for wrecking my project yesterday but OF COURSE NOT. She's Miranda Maroni. It's ALWAYS all about HER.

If she's not talking nonstop about all of her STUFF, she's going on and on about her performance at the last volleyball game. Everyone in class has to hear about how many points she scored, how many balls she spiked, and blah, blah, blah. IT. NEVER. ENDS.

Of course, Miranda wouldn't even have all those spikes if it weren't for Emily, who usually sets up the ball for her. If you ask me, Emily is the MVP of the team.

I got in a bad mood all over again just thinking about Miranda. **DID I SAY HOW GLAD I AM THAT IT'S FRIDAY?**

I tried so hard to get through the day without griping and instead keep my nose buried in my sketchbook. I've got a great idea for an apron for Sophie. She's always cooking up something in the kitchen, so she needs a Catie Conrad fashion accessory to protect her clothes.

I could hardly wait to get home and be by myself for a while. I closed the door, laid on my bed, listened to my favorite music, and said my prayers. Then I got to work on cutting out fabric for Sophie's apron. Whenever Mom sees fabric on sale, she buys a few yards of something she thinks I might like. Sophie's favorite color is orange, so I picked out a fruity print in orange and pink, and I'm going to paint an orange S on the pocket. I can't wait to see her face when I finally finish it. ☺

Of course, I won't give it to Sophie if Miranda is standing by anywhere close. I'd be laughed out of sixth grade. ☹

I also have a SUPER idea for a new dress! Well, the dress is only sort of new, but it will look ABSOLUTELY NEW when I'm finished with it. ☺ I got it at a vintage shop in town for just THREE dollars! By the time I change the sleeves and make a new belt, it will look AWESOME. Sketching my ideas always helps get my mind off things—those things being Miranda . . . AND the school dance.

BTW, my Prayer List is getting
Loooonnnggerr and Loooonnnggerr.
And Miranda is at the very **TOP**!
☹ TTYL . . .

Mom got home Late from work . . . AGAIN. Between her work and Dad being hoLed up in his office, it's hard to see my famiLy aLL at the same time. But I couLd teLL Mom was totaLLy stressed out. Something about "having a grouchy patient who didn't want to get a shot in her mouth." WHO WOULD?

Mom works at a dentist office for kids and assists Dr. HamiLton with aLL the patients. I can't imagine deaLing with that aLL day. Mom has to caLm down screaming kids one minute and assist Dr. HamiLton with the tooLs of doom the next. When I'm forced to go there, I cLose my eyes when Dr. HamiLton comes at me wearing that mask and hoLding a creepy instrument. It's Like something out of a HORROR movie!

Maybe since Mom's in a bad mood too, we won't be having a **S.A.D.** night—or at least that's what I secretly call it. These are nights where we all have to **S**it **A**t **D**inner and tell something good about our day.

UGH.

Sometimes it can be fun, but today was NOT one of them.

God, pLease don't Let it be a **S.A.D.** night!

I'm way too upset over Miranda and this dumb school dance to try and make up something good about my day. And I CERTAINLY don't feel like looking at the Germ and Rosey any more than I have to. That crazy skunk is ready to pounce on any morsel of food, 24/7. Why should that crazy animal be allowed around the dinner table in the first place? **WHY???**

I'd rather just relax and eat dinner in front of the TV. Maybe I can block the art disaster and Miranda out of my mind with a good show.

Of course, the Germ will turn it to HIS favorite channel and get HIS way because HE'S the baby. (SO NOT FAIR.) I'LL be forced to watch the Animal Channel and hear about some weird freak of nature like a fainting goat or a Japanese spider crab. **UGH!!!!!!!!!!!!!!**

GTG! I just heard Mom yell that dinner's ready. . . .
  More L8R!

YES!!!! Mom caved tonight and said the Germ and I could sit on the sofa and have pizza for dinner. ☺ ☺ ☺

I hurried to the kitchen and made sure I got a nice juicy slice of pepperoni before the Germ and Rosey moved in on it.

YUM!

Luckily, I was just in time for the best show ever: Fashion Star Fever!

Each week a young designer gets to create fashions for a runway show. If the judges really like it and give it a high score, they actually BUY the designs and sell them at a department store!! **CAN YOU IMAGINE?** I might pass out if I saw someone walking down the street wearing an outfit I'd designed. No, I KNOW I would pass out!

Just as I got cozy on the couch and was ready to watch my show, the Germ stormed into the Living room with Rosey. He grabbed the TV remote and turned it to some weird show called The Giant Rodents of South America.

UGHHHHHHHHHHHH!!!!!!!!

Me: Okay, so WHY are we watching this? You KNOW it's time for my favorite show. I'm teLLing Mom!

YUCK!

Jeremy: Who wants to watch your goofy show about goofy clothes? It's dumb. Tonight they're featuring a giant rodent called a CAPYBARA! Know what that is? It's a GIANT GUINEA PIG! They have three toes on their rear feet and four toes on their front feet! They're also semi-aquatic so they can live in the water or out—like in or out of my bathtub! Maybe I can talk Mom and Dad into buying me one! The people on Animal Planet say they can become very cuddly and territorial if you train them.

Me: HAVE YOU LOST YOUR MIND? That DOES IT! I'm going to my room! I'M OUTTA HERE!

When I told Mom and Dad what the Germ had done, they griped at ME for yelling at him. I couldn't believe it! Sometimes I wish I was an only child. At least I wouldn't have to worry about what type of gross animal will be brought into our house next!

I went straight to my room, got out my diary, and added the GERM and a CAPYBARA to my Prayer List.

GOD,
PLEASE
DO NOT LET A
GIANT GUINEA PIG BE
IN MY FUTURE!

I also rummaged around in my room to find artsy materials to try and save my RUINED project. Of course that reminded me of Miranda, and I suddenly got S.A.D. for real. ☹ ☹

SATURDAY, MARCH 20

If Mom REALLY wanted me to be nice to the Germ (so nice that she probably wouldn't even recognize me), then she'd tell Dad how much I DESPERATELY need a new cell phone! I'm the only kid in class who has a phone that came over on Noah's ark. YES, it is that OLD.

Mom gave me her old one, when, of course, SHE got the upgrade phone that has the latest and greatest of everything. It has a zillion free apps, which she has NO CLUE how to download or use! Why would Mom need that?

WHY???

But no, Catie Conrad gets the phone that doesn't even connect to the Internet! **WHO DOES THAT TO A KID?** I'll tell you who. The kind of parents who buy two diaries full of blank paper and expect their kid to actually WRITE in it! Don't they know it's the twenty-first century?

Maybe SOMEDAY they'll understand, but I'm not holding my breath.

.UGH.

High Tech Phone + MOM = DOUBLE WEIRD

High Tech Phone + Catie Conrad = INSTANT COOLNESS!

(Extra bonus points if I get a blinged-out case! ☺ ☺ ☺ ☺)

I've decided to wait until after dinner (so Mom has time to "de-stress") to explain WHY I need a new cell phone. To wow her, I might actually create a PowerPoint presentation later to really help get the point across.

WHY CATIE
DESERVES
A NEW PHONE

UGH. Obviously I didn't wait long enough . . .

Me: Uh, Mom, SINCE I'm going to bed on time and SINCE I've said my prayers every night, do you think we could talk about something? I really, REALLY need a new cell phone. Sophie just got one, and it's awesome. You can ask her mom about it if you'd like.

Mom: Catie, while I appreciate you going to bed on time and saying your prayers, that doesn't mean you're going to get everything you want, when you want it. We can't afford a new phone for you right now, sweetie. Remember, we're trying to save money for the overseas missionaries who need supplies. The phone that you have is fine. You're not supposed to be on the phone at school anyway. When you're at home, you can call Sophie from the house phone, the old-fashioned way. What's wrong with that?

Upset Me: But Mooommmm! That's the problem—it's OLD-FASHIONED! It's not fair! I have the ugliest phone in the whole class. I'm really trying to be good! When you ask me to be nice to the Germ, er, I mean, Jeremy, I really TRY. My grades are great, er well, good—not a single C! I even make up my bed almost every morning! Surely that deserves SOMETHING!

Mom: Catie Conrad, just because we think we deserve something, it doesn't mean God is going to allow it to happen in the snap of a finger. You know better than that, right? What happened to being nice and doing your best because it's the right thing to do? Maybe you can use some of your allowance savings to buy yourself a phone. We're done discussing this now. You can think about it, and we'll revisit this issue. Time for bed. I love you very much.

Me: ☹ ☹ ☹ ☹

PRAYER LIST: Pray for contentment . . . AGAIN!!!!!

SUNDAY, MARCH 21

Even though I'm still mad at Mom for saying NO to a modern cell phone, something happened in church today that made me glad I didn't have one. (At least for today.)

Sophie had been talking on her cell to her cousin, right before church started. HOWEVER, when she threw the phone into her purse, she forgot to put it on silent! Unfortunately, her cousin decided to call back—RIGHT DURING PRAYER. Talk about BAD TIMING!

Just as we were about to say amen, everyone suddenly heard the ringtone "I LIKE TO MOVE IT MOVE IT!" from that Madagascar movie. Every head in church turned to look at Sophie.

Sophie's face turned every color of red that was humanly possible. I FELT SO BAD FOR HER. I've never seen Sophie scramble so hard to open her purse and turn off that phone.

Of course, the Germ thought it was funny, and I noticed him lying on his side giggling in the pew behind me. I have a feeling Sophie will start praying for patience with my crazy brother as much as I do!

So chic! ♡

With the exception of the phone incident, church was really interesting today. A lady from Spirit Ministries, the group Dad is writing an article about, came and talked about mission work in the Southwest, especially at Native American reservations. I didn't realize that an area in my own country could be so different! I couldn't imagine living in a desert or seeing cactuses everywhere. That would be so AWESOME. At least Miranda Maroni wouldn't be anywhere around!

SINCE I'm a fashion designer, and SINCE I'LL be designing clothes for PEOPLE aLL over the country, I decided to do a GoogLe search for "SOUTHWEST FASHIONS" as soon as I got home from church.

My search turned UP aLL kinds of images! Cowboys boots! CoLorfuL skirts and cooL jean jackets! Southwest fashions totaLLy rock! And WOW, when I checked out "NATIVE AMERICAN OUTFITS," there were incredibLe costumes in every coLor of the rainbow.

I spent the rest of the afternoon drawing Catie Conrad versions of Southwest fashions. Who knows, I might even create my very own Line of cowboy boots one of these days!

72

After dinner, I showed Mom and Dad my fashion sketches, and even they thought they were cool. Dad also told us that he'd spoken to the lady from Spirit Ministries after church. He was so moved by her presentation that he volunteered our family to go to Arizona and host Vacation Bible School at an Apache reservation in a few weeks. Evidently it will be during spring break for the kids on the rez, and Dad feels so strongly about it that he thinks it's even worth me and Jeremy missing school for a few days.

I think he said we're going on April 6, which isn't too far away.

WAIT A MINUTE . . . WAIT A MINUTE . . .
APRIL 6th? **THAT'S JUST TEN DAYS BEFORE THE BIG DANCE!**
I have a zillion things to do before then!

1. Try and save my mosaic from being a total **FLOP**.
2. Finish a few of the fashion designs I started.
3. Find a dress for the school dance. Because if some—
   body—Josh!—asks me, I have to be ready to go, right?

MONDAY, MARCH 22

It was so hard to go to school today and look Miranda in the face. The only thing I could think of when I looked at her was my messed-up project and beads bouncing all over the floor. ☹

Unless I figure out how to fix my project and FAST, I'm looking at a big fat C in art class. ☹ ☹ ☹ ☹

At least it won't be an F. However, a C in our house stands for CAN do better.

UGH . . .

Miranda even had the nerve to try and SPEAK to me this morning on the way to her locker, which is just three down from mine and Sophie's. I mumbled a quick, "Hey Miranda" and slammed my locker door. I concentrated on talking to Sophie.

But suddenly I forgot what I was doing when I heard Mrs. Gibson's voice over the school intercom:

Mrs. Gibson: Students, I'm delighted to announce that our school has decided to host its first ever Middle School Art Show. There are several categories to choose from, so check out the big poster in the art room. The top honor, "Best in Show," will receive a beautiful plaque, $25, and ten bonus points in art class. Good luck everyone and remember: ART RULES!

I could hardly wait to talk to Sophie about this! Even though the contest wasn't until the end of April, I needed to GET STARTED NOW.

Me: There's only ONE way to bring up my art grade and that's to win this art contest. If I keep a C in art class, I AM DOOMED. Oh, and did I mention Dad is making us go on a mission trip in a few weeks? Talk about BAD TIMING.

Sophie: Why do we ALL have to enter something for the art contest? Everyone knows you're the best artist at school. Now, if this were a SCIENCE fair, then I'd be all over it. But what am I supposed to do for an art contest? That's just weird. Oh, and the mission trip sounds fun if you ask me.

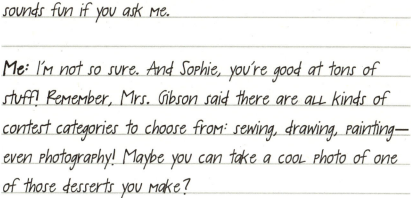

Me: I'm not so sure. And Sophie, you're good at tons of stuff! Remember, Mrs. Gibson said there are all kinds of contest categories to choose from: sewing, drawing, painting—even photography! Maybe you can take a cool photo of one of those desserts you make?

Sophie: Or that would be just W-E-I-R-D. Art just isn't my thing. I bet I can guess what category you'll be entering—sewing, right? I can't wait to see what kind of fancy fashion design you'll come up with for the contest.

Just when I was about to tell Sophie that I didn't plan on entering the sewing category, Miranda had to put her two cents in. She'd been standing at her locker with Emily and listening to the whole thing: "Are you STILL convinced you're a fashion designer? **Really?** Well, Catie Conrad, if you ever need a model, just let me know. I'm available."

And on that last word she waltzed down the hall with her ponytail flipping in the air.

UGH! SHE DRIVES ME BONKERS!

On top of everything else going on in my crazy life, I had to go to science class—my worst subject ever. ☹

At least Sophie was my partner today. Mr. Finkleman (yes, that is his ACTUAL name!) made us choose a lab partner, and I'd chosen my best friend. I wondered who in the world would choose Miranda. But then I noticed she was standing by Emily—AGAIN.

OF COURSE.

Maybe if Miranda had destroyed HER art project, she wouldn't be as understanding.

Mr. Finkleman's lecture about cells made **ZERO SENSE** to me. NADA, ZILCH, NOTHING.

I couldn't understand a single thing!

Sophie seemed to actually LIKE this stuff and wrote down every word he said. STRANGE! Maybe she could translate it all to me later.

I DO NOT like science and wonder why ANYONE needs to know what a cell looks like—something we can't even see!

Like I said, STRANGE!

Mr. Finkleman drew a diagram of a cell on the board and made us do the same thing in our notebooks. We had to label every single part, which seemed like a total waste of good sketch paper. Why couldn't we label plants, like we did in fourth grade?

But then Mr. Finkleman REALLY dropped a bomb:

"Class, your new assignment is to create your very own version of a cell and label it accordingly. You can work on it as a team, and it's due in two days. Good luck! Think out of the box and be super creative!"

HUH???

What kind of teacher would dream up such a crazy project? And why would he only give us two days to complete it? GIMME A BREAK!

I hoped Sophie had an idea because I was CLUELESS. ALL I could think about was the big art contest just a few weeks away. I HAD TO HAVE AN IDEA AND FAST!

Luckily, Sophie was already making a TO-DO list for our science project. I told you she was smart! However, this time I thought she'd lost her marbles . . .

Sophie: I've got it! We can make a cell out of JELL-O! It's the perfect ingredient!

Me: JELL-O? For a science project? Tell me it's not going to turn out like one of those spa experiments? That could spell D-I-S-A-S-T-E-R.

Sophie: Trust me. Come over after school tomorrow and bring the things on this list with you. This is going to be SO COOL!

I'm glad my brainiac BFF thought so . . .

Add to Prayer List:

1. Pray that I can come up with an idea for the Middle School Art Show.

2. Pray that I won't wreck our big science project!

TUESDAY, MARCH 23

I can't believe I have to work on a boring science project after school today. I'd much rather focus on art and coming up with an idea for the contest. If my friends knew that I had ZERO inspiration and was totally brain blocked, they'd laugh me off the planet.

And that includes Josh Henderson. The only time he even notices me is when I draw something cool in art class.

WELL, NOT ANYMORE!

My days of being Catie Conrad, the A+ art student are O-V-E-R. ☹

At least I'll be working on my science project with Sophie. I'm glad SOMEONE had an idea in her head! However, I think she may have gone over the edge after looking at the list of stuff she'd given me to get at the grocery. It looked way more like ingredients for one of her recipes—NOT A SCIENCE PROJECT.

CATIE'S LIST

Miniature marshmallows

Licorice straw

Large gumball

SOPHIE'S LIST

Lemon JELL-O

Sour candy and roll-up fruit snacks

Sturdy plastic bag to hold the JELL-O

I texted Dad and asked him to stop by the grocery and bring home the things on my list. Notice I said TEXTED Dad—Sophie was nice enough to let me use HER cell phone because I DON'T HAVE ONE THAT TEXTS. I made a mental note to add that to my list of why I need a new phone. Surely reason #27, NEED FOR IMPORTANT SCHOOL STUFF, would clinch the deal.

By the time I got to Sophie's, she had everything set out on the kitchen counter. Utensils, pots, pans, and all sorts of ingredients were everywhere. It looked like some crazy science lab!

86

Sophie also had on the apron I made for her. ☺ It fit perfectly, and she even had on an orange T-shirt to match. It looked awesome! At least there's ONE person at school who believes in me!

I followed Sophie's lead on what to do next and tried not to mess up anything. I could tell my BFF knew exactly what she was doing.

We mixed the JELL-O with water and poured it into the plastic bag—that was the cell wall. The JELL-O stuff was the cytoplasm, and the large gumball was the nucleus. As it jelled in the fridge, we added the different types of candy to look like the different parts of the cell: vacuole, ribosomes, lysosomes, golgi body, and mitochondrion. This was way harder than those baking soda volcanoes I used to make!

I'll have to admit, though, it's pretty cool how God creates so many interesting parts to every living thing. What an imagination! Like the song says: HE IS AMAZING!

Maybe cells are starting to make sense a little . . .

Mr. Finkleman is going to LOVE this! I'm letting Sophie be in charge of bringing it to school tomorrow. It was her idea, after all.

NOTE TO SELF:

KEEP MIRANDA AWAY FROM OUR PROJECT!!!

I spent the rest of the afternoon looking for mosaic pieces for my sewing machine project. Art class was just a few days away, and it was our last day to finish it. At least Mrs. Gibson had been nice enough to let us bring home our project. I racked my brain for hours trying to come up with something. FINALLY Mom came to the rescue!

Brilliant Mom: Hey Catie, how about using some of those old plastic bobbin spools that you don't use anymore? Some of them still have a little thread left so they might give your mosaic some color.

88

Thankful Me: Mom, you're a GENIUS! Now I know for SURE where I get my art genes. That's a great idea.

Amazing Mom: And I think your dad may have some tile left from when we remodeled the bathroom. Maybe he can cut them into tiny pieces to fill in?

I had no time to waste and quickly got the tweezers and glue. Anything would be an improvement since my project only had a few black beads stuck on it here and there. I ever so gently filled in my drawing with the plastic bobbins and blue tile. It looked so cool, if I have to say so myself. I planned on hanging it up in my bedroom once Mrs. Gibson graded it. It might not be the best mosaic in class, but hopefully it can help pull my grade up from a C to an A.

And if I'm REALLY lucky, JOSH MIGHT EVEN LIKE IT! Then my cramped fingers would totally be worth it!

Add to Prayer List:

1. Thank God for giving me a best friend like Sophie Martin. ☺
2. Thank God for giving me such a creative mom!

WEDNESDAY, MARCH 24

I was right: Mr. Finkleman LOVED OUR SCIENCE PROJECT! YES! YES! YES!

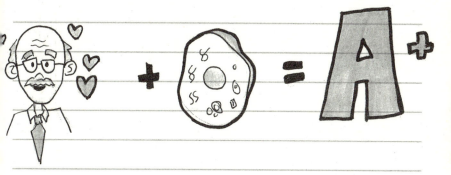

And guess what? Miranda wasn't even at school today, so we didn't have to worry that she might "accidentally" bump into it and cause a disaster.
YES!!!

I overheard Emily tell Sophie that Miranda was sort of stressed out about something. Well MAYBE it's because she's finally thought about how rude she acts to everyone.
But what am I thinking? She's probably just upset that she doesn't have every single item in *Teen Vogue* this month.
SHEESH!!

After getting a glorious A+ on our science project (THANK YOU, SOPHIE!), we decided to take it over to my house and celebrate in the perfect way: EAT IT !!!

But instead of worrying about Miranda wrecking our project at school, I SHOULD have been thinking about the REAL threat at my own house:

THE GERM!!!!!!!!!!!

In the amount of time it took us to set our project on the table and get a soda out of the fridge, the Germ's pest of a pet had hopped up and STUCK HER BIG FAT NOSE IN OUR JELL-O CELL!

GRRRRRR . . .

In two seconds, Rosey had a Fruit Roll-Up hanging out of her mouth. Marshmallows were stuck all over her tail, and she looked like a total freak.

And the WORST part about the whole thing was THE
GERM THOUGHT IT WAS CUTE!
NOT!!! NO WAY!!! NO HOW!!!

No wonder Sophie
never comes to my
house.
    Maybe I can move
in with her!

    It was all I could
do to even be
remotely nice to the
Germ tonight. And to
make matters worse,
it was a S.A.D. night!

UGH!!!!!

What was with Mom and these weird dinner table rules?

At least she was fixing one of my favorite meals: spaghetti and meatballs with garlic bread. DELISH.

I'm convinced we're part Italian because Mom makes the best meatballs of anyone I know. And since I LOVE Italian food, I'm sure part of our family must be from Rome— RIGHT? Maybe that's where I get my fashion flair? The Italians definitely have as much style as the designers in Paris. Maybe I'll be on the cover of one of those Italian magazines too!

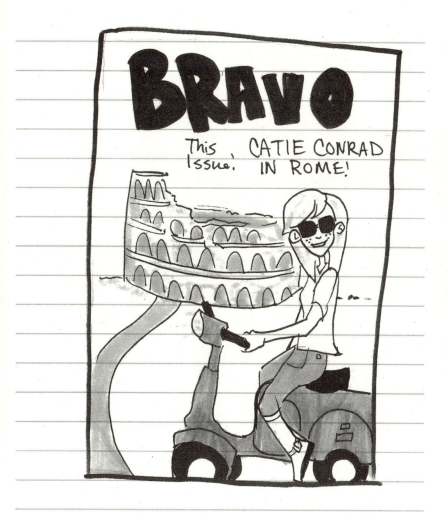

When Mom finally called us to dinner, it was just as I'd suspected: **STINK BOMB ROSEY** had to be my brother's little shadow around the table. Maybe I'll eat extra garlic bread and then breathe on the Germ after dinner. That's the only comeback I have since I don't have a gross pet that reeks!

Mom: I hope everyone had a super day and is ready to share something good! I took our pastor's advice and invited one of our patient's family to church! They're new to the neighborhood and going to try to visit this Sunday. I said we'd love to have them sit with us. Right, gang?

Dad: That's wonderful, dear! My good news is I just got our plane tickets for the mission trip to Arizona. I thought you and the kids might want to be in charge of the VBS crafts. Catie, didn't I see you working on a mosaic yesterday? Maybe the Native American kids would enjoy something like that.

Me: I'd LOVE to help with crafts! Only my mosaic didn't turn out so well. But Mom's idea helped out BIG TIME. As for good news today . . . hmmm . . . I guess my good news is I got an A+ on Mr. Finkleman's cell assignment! That's all I can think of—UNLESS you'd like to SEE my science project? ISN'T THAT RIGHT, ROSEY?

The GERM: You are SO mean, Catie! Okay, I'll admit it. Rosey tried to eat Catie's project. But it was made out of

CANDY and JELL-O, for crying out loud! Even I took a bite! Sorry, Catie, but Rosey is an omnivore, so she'll try anything! She must have thought that Fruit Roll-Up was a salamander or something.

Me: Then you need to get that skunk's eyes checked!

Dad: Okay, that's enough you two. Tell your sister you're sorry, Jeremy Conrad. You need to keep that skunk under control.

The GERM: Sorry, Catie. . . . (MUMBLING SO LOW THAT I COULD BARELY HEAR HIM.)

I am STILL soooooo mad at the Germ and Rosey, but I have to forgive them I guess. ☹ ☹ ☹ ☹ ☹

AHH!

BUT IT'S CERTAINLY NOT GOING TO BE EASY!!!!!

At least the spaghetti was good. Actually, it was more like DELICIOSO! Just when I was about to forgive the pest for eating my project, I looked over and saw him and the Germ SHARING a spaghetti noodle! YES, that's what I said—THEY WERE SLURPING ON A SPAGHETTI NOODLE—just like the dogs on that Disney movie!

GROSS!!!!

WHO WANTS SKUNK SPIT ON HIS FOOD?
MY BROTHER HAS OFFICIALLY LOST IT!

THURSDAY, MARCH 25

I could hardly keep my eyes open on the way to school today. I was so excited to finally have time to work on fashion designs last night that I lost track of time and stayed up tooooo late. If only I liked coffee like my parents!

Instead, I felt like a **TOTAL ZOMBIE.**

I had to snap out of it because today I had ART CLASS! Mom had carefully wrapped my project in plastic—thank goodness. I'd told her about Miranda INTENTIONALLY bumping into it last week.

Mom: Try to overlook her if at all possible, Catie.

EASY FOR HER TO SAY. ☹

When I got to class, Mrs. Gibson had cleared off the back table so we'd have room to display our projects. Miranda had made her volleyball out of pearl beads (of course!), and Sophie's project turned out nicer than I'd expected. She'd filled in her cross with all sorts of seashells, and it was beautiful. Josh had done a mosaic of his dog, Jasper, and used black licorice pieces for the fur.

If only Josh knew how much I loved dogs, we'd be the perfect match for sure. Hey, I even like black licorice!

I breathed a sigh of relief when Mrs. Gibson said I'd done a great job. WHEW! She really liked the bobbin idea and said it should help my grade.

THIS WAS THE BEST DAY EVER!!!!!!
THAT IS, UNTIL P.E.

Have I ever written in this diary how much I hate P.E. class? Well, I DO! I'd rather babysit Rosey than go to P.E.
YES, IT'S THAT BAD!!!

It was especially a BUMMER today, but let me explain. . . .

Coach Calloway (who's always in some kind of neon glow-in-the-dark jogging suit) had the brilliant idea to talk about "Healthy Eating Habits for the twenty-first Century."

Eeh.

Not only were our school cafeteria meals the farthest thing from tasty (and I mean MILES and MILES from tasty!), but our coach also had a tableful of food that he ORDERED us to sample. He even said he'd dock our grade if we refused to try it.

TALK ABOUT TORTURE!

So here are the things he set out on the table: broccoli, tomatoes, pears, blueberries, and cheese. GROSS. GROSS. DOUBLE GROSS.

"Growing boys and girls like you need fruits and vegetables!" he said. "You need to eat at least four to six servings per day. They're full of vitamins and are DELISH!"

The girls in our class stood around the table and stared. I even noticed that Miranda and Emily didn't look too happy about it.

The boys, on the other hand, couldn't have cared less. They started devouring everything. I've never seen Josh Henderson eat like that! Not only is he handsome and smart, but he even EATS healthy! UNBELIEVABLE!

Sophie didn't mind trying all that stuff either. I guess I shouldn't be surprised since she cooks all the time. With that smile on her face, you would have thought she was eating cotton candy.

NOT ME! Why broccoli even exists on earth, I have no clue.

WHY WOULD ANYONE WANT TO EAT RAW TREES?

And blueberries? Sorry, but the texture is just too weird. They taste like squashed bugs. I couldn't stand it and had to spit them out onto a napkin. And the worst of all was the tomato. GROOOOSSSS . . . The ONLY way I can eat them is if they're drowned in ranch dressing, and I didn't see a bottle of it anywhere.

"The flesh of a tomato is filled with nutrients!" said Coach. "And this one is extra juicy!"

Flesh of a tomato? Did he have to use those words? I felt like a cannibal eating a piece of human flesh. Ewww . . .

Miranda and Emily weren't trying much of the stuff either. "I'm not a fan of pears," I overheard Miranda say to Emily. "It tastes like I'm eating wet sand. That's just disgusting."

I couldn't believe I agreed with Miranda on something. Of course, I didn't tell her that.

BUT then Coach said something that REALLY caused me to pay attention—in a GOOD way: "Try some of the fruit and cheese together. The white cheese is called brie. Just think, kids all over the world love this treat . . . especially the French."

WHAT? The only cheese I like is grilled. But if girls in the FASHION CAPITAL OF THE WORLD like this stuff, COUNT ME IN!

Bonjour!

I could only imagine sitting on a balcony in Paris, sketching a fabulous outfit, and nibbling on fruit and cheese.

Ooh La La!!!! Ooh La La!!! Ooh La La!!!

If only that was all I had to sample. I couldn't possibly afford to get a bad grade in P.E. Another bad grade would doom me for all eternity.

I had no choice but to try all of the other junk too. ☹ ☹

I held my nose on the broccoli but got it down somehow. Whoever said that holding your nose keeps you from tasting anything was **INSANE.**

If I had to eat broccoli to stay alive, I would have been dead by now.

The rest of my day went **WAAAAAY DOWNHILL** from there. ☹ ☹ ☹ When the bell finally rang, everyone hurried on to art class. I could hardly wait to get a drink of water and wash that tree taste out of my mouth.

BUT THEN IT HAPPENED: Josh was walking right BEHIND me in the hallway! Sophie gave me "the look," like I should at least turn around and say hi to him.

But. I. FROZE. . . . My BRAIN WENT **TOTALLY** NUMB.

OH, AND THAT'S JUST THE HALF OF IT. While I was still in zombie mode, Josh suddenly SPOKE TO ME! "Hey, Catie," he said, "that was one weird P.E. class today, huh?"

I couldn't think of a single thing to say. **I JUST STOOD THERE AND STARED.**

Luckily, Sophie saved the day: "Uh, yeah, Josh, totally weird!" she said. "Catie and I were just talking about that. Right, Catie? RIGHT, CATIE?"

"Oh, uh, right! You can say that again, Josh!" I said, smiling at him from ear to ear. I was finally learning how to put a sentence together without sounding like a total idiot. I even remembered to smile. ☺ Shocking.

THEN Josh suddenly gave me the strangest look ever. He zoomed around me as fast as he could and joined up with Tyler.

HUH? WHAT WAS WITH HIM???

"What did I say?" I asked, turning to Sophie. "ALL I did was agree with him that P.E. was weird. I can't do anything right! What is wrong with me?"

But suddenly Sophie looked at me with an even stranger look. WHAT WAS WITH EVERYONE?

"Uh, Catie, I think I need to show you something," Sophie said, quickly pulling me into the bathroom.

Now I was REALLY starting to get nervous. I was almost positive I'd put on deodorant this morning. Or maybe I had bad breath? I made a mental note to pack some breath mints in my backpack tomorrow.

Sophie turned me around and stuck my face toward the mirror. **OH. MY. GOSH.** I had a *GINORMOUS* piece of broccoli wedged between my front teeth!!!! IT WAS HORRIBLE!!!!!!!!!

No wonder Josh bolted past me in two seconds. Why on EARTH would he want to talk to a girl with a green shrub stuck between her teeth?

I CAN NEVER LOOK AT JOSH HENDERSON AGAIN AS LONG AS I LIVE.

I quickly dug the hunk of green out of my teeth. If only I could stay in the bathroom for the rest of the day . . . or better yet, **FOR THE REST OF MY LIFE!**

But just as I turned the corner on my way to my next class, BOOM, I ran RIGHT INTO MRS. GIBSON, knocking the container of paintbrushes out of her hand.

I AM SUCH A KLUTZ!

Mrs. Gibson could tell I was TOTALLY upset.

Besides my parents and Sophie, Mrs. Gibson knows me better than anyone. "Are you okay today, Catie?" she asked. "You know if you ever need to talk to someone, you can talk to me."

I wanted to reach over and give Mrs. Gibson the biggest hug ever.

But I didn't.

It was just my luck that someone in the hall would see me and call me a big baby.

A BABY WITH BROCCOLI BREATH.

FRIDAY, MARCH 26

I am SO READY for this week to be OVER. My chance of going to the dance is ZILCH!!!!!!!!

Luckily, there was zero drama at school today. Well, ALMOST zero drama . . .

This time it was all because of my dumb backpack, which happens to weigh as much as a small car. Maybe I should design a back-pack that doesn't cause my spine to feel like it's going to snap!

Besides having six teachers and TONS of homework, being in middle school means having a locker on the other side of the planet. I have no choice but to cram every book I'll need for the ENTIRE day into my backpack. Perhaps Mom was right: carrying around a heavy backpack was going to turn me into a hunchback—a definite no-go for a fashion designer.

Today I'd also packed a mirror, toothbrush, toothpaste, breath mints, and dental floss—just in case there was another dental disaster. I quickly rushed into the bathroom to double check my teeth.

That's when I came face-to-face with MIRANDA and EMILY. I couldn't risk Miranda seeing me check my teeth for grossness. THANK GOODNESS she was too busy spraying her hair and reapplying her ten pounds of makeup. Sometimes Miranda lays it on a little thick. Scratch that—she does that ALL the time!

Mom and Dad only allow me to wear lip gloss and powder, but of course I ask to wear more. After all, makeup and fashions go hand in hand! But this morning, after watching Miranda primp, I decided to get out my watermelon-flavored lip gloss and make sure my hair didn't look weird.

"Hey Catie," said Emily. "I like that flavor of lip gloss too. Mom bought me some just like that last week."

Miranda didn't say a single thing. **NATURALLY.**

Just as I was about to say hi to Emily, I heaved my ginormous backpack onto the sink counter. In two seconds, the zipper broke, SPILLING EVERTHING out of my backpack. ☹

And of course, Miranda had to be the one to bend over and pick up my toothbrush, dental floss, and breath mints. ☹ ☹ ☹

OF COURSE SHE DID.

But to my surprise, she just handed them back to me without saying anything rude.

WEIRD. What was wrong with her? Maybe Miranda has one of those split personalities? She probably talked about me behind my back as soon as I left.

BUT AT LEAST IT'S FRIDAY! YES!! YES!!! YES!!!!

I'm determined to quit thinking about the dance—AND Miranda—AND Josh!

WeLL, I'm going to TRY at Least. . . .

Tonight was so cooL for a ZILLION reasons:

1. Dad took us to our favorite Italian restaurant for dinner—Deliciozo Italiano. He even said Sophie couLd come aLong too. ☺

Deliciozo Italiano!

$ Gift Card $

2. The Germ had to Leave Rosey at home because we were eating at a nice restaurant. HAHAHAHAHAH!!!!!

3. Sophie got to sLeep over. First we talked about the dance. Sophie says she's going, and she wants me to go too. I'LL have to think about that since I'm stiLL HOPING that Josh asks me. ☺ Then we created some new spa recipes (her favorite thing to do) and designed amazing outfits (my favorite thing to do) untiL 12 AM! *IT WAS AWESOME!*

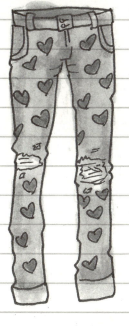

Pink Sugar Body Scrub

Ingredients: 1 cup sugar, 1 cup honey, 1 teaspoon strawberry extract, 1/2 teaspoon vanilla extract, 3 tablespoons baby oil, pink food coloring, 1 small jar or container with lid.

Step 1: In a mixing bowl, combine sugar, honey, extracts, and baby oil. Mix well until all ingredients are blended.

Step 2: Add a small amount of pink food coloring, and stir.

Step 3: Spoon mixture into jar or container. Store for one week.

I also gave Sophie a diary of her own since she'd mentioned mine was kinda cool. She even said she's going to keep a Prayer List, just like I do. ☺

I asked Sophie to write down our family's name ASAP. Our mission trip was coming up, and we had no clue what working at an Indian rez would be like. We needed all the prayer we could get!

Who knows, maybe the Germ and I might get to hang out with Apache kids our own age. That could be VERY COOL.
   OR

That could be **VERY STRANGE**...

   I wonder if Native American girls wear the same fashions as Sophie and I?

   I wonder if they keep weird diaries?

   I wonder if any of them like art as much as I do?

   Maybe I'll look that stuff up later on the Internet...

   G' NIGHT!!!!

SATURDAY, MARCH 27

FINALLY . . . THE WEEKEND!!!!
WOOT! WOOT! WOOT!

I have NO homework, NOTHING to do, and I plan on staying in my p.j.'s THE ENTIRE DAY! YES!

I've got everything planned: turn on my favorite music, lounge on my bed, and draw fashions in my sketchbook as long as I want! I might not even brush my hair—or my teeth. ☺

I LOVE SATURDAY!

Correction: I am SUPPOSED to love Saturdays. . . . ☹ ☹ ☹

Is there such a thing as a CREEP-A-ZOID?

If it's in the dictionary, then I'm sure there's a picture of my eight-year-old brother right beside it.

CREEP–A–ZOID:

1. One who reeks of wet skunk or moldy garbage.
2. Someone who eats EVERY SINGLE potato chip in the bag and then leaves the bag in the cabinet to psych me out.
3. Someone who hogs the computer just so he can watch videos about weird animals like the two-toed sloth or star-nosed mole. (WHO CARES!)
4. Anyone named JEREMY "The GERM" CONRAD.

TO DO LIST:
PRAY FOR PATIENCE
WHEN DEALING WITH
THE CREEP–A–ZOID!

This Saturday morning (which, again, was SUPPOSED to be a relaxing day), the Germ would NOT LEAVE ME ALONE.

"If you put even a single TOENAIL into my room, you are DEAD MEAT!" I warned him. "Not only do you smell like a garbage can, but there is NO WAY you're getting within breathing distance of my drawings."

The Germ quietly slid one foot inside my room, staring straight at me. He even wiggled his big TOE, acting like a **TOTAL BRAT!**

As long as the Germ's black and white creature still roams the Earth, my room is totally **OFF LIMITS!** Why my brother threw a total tantrum over wanting a pet skunk, I have NO CLUE. I personally think he'd been eating school glue when he asked Dad for one, but I can't prove it.

"But *DAAAADDDD,*" he whined like a big baby, "vets can take the smelly gland out so it won't stink. I saw them do it on Animal Planet! I can walk him on a leash, and he can even ride in the car with us on the way to school. Pleeeeeease!"

Blah, blah, blah . . .

I still can't believe Dad fell for it! Rosey (who would name a skunk Rosey?) even has her own bed. He and the Germ probably have matching pajamas for all I know.

WEIRD. WEIRD.
DOUBLE WEIRD!!!

And riding to school is a **TOTAL NIGHTMARE**. If only Mom's van had tinted windows. I'm forced to sit in the back and hide while the Germ looks like a total freak riding in the front and holding that dumb skunk in his lap. He even keeps the windows rolled down so that Rosey can hang her head out like a dog.

The Germ says skunks like to feel the wind in their fur, but I don't buy it for a second. I think he's afraid that there's some part of that STINK gland left and Rosey might do a major backfire on him!

To make my Saturday even worse, I got grounded because my room was "a total disaster area"—or so Mom said. She was right, I guess. I couldn't find my favorite earrings or my sketchbook—which I TOTALLY need in order to work on my art project.

I spent the rest of my wrecked Saturday at home with the Germ . . . and THE STINK BOMB. ☹ ☹

The ONLY good thing that happened was I FINALLY CAME UP WITH AN AWESOME IDEA FOR THE SCHOOL ART CONTEST!

YES! YES! YES!

It will take A LOT of work to make my drawing PERFECT, but it's worth a shot. After sketching and erasing a GAZILLION times, my idea slowly came together. It's très chic:

If only I could be on *Fashion Star Fever!* Then I'd become a millionaire and never have to go to school again!

SUNDAY, MARCH 28

I can't believe it—the family Mom invited to church actually showed up and sat with us. They just moved to town and seemed pretty cool. Their daughter, Sarah, was the Germ's age and seemed eager to talk to him. (I SHOULD HAVE WARNED HER!) It didn't take but two seconds for my goofy brother to show her a pic of that dumb skunk. WHAT A NERD.

They also have a son named Tyler who's enrolling in my class tomorrow. He barely said a word to me in church, but that didn't shock me. I'm beginning to think that **ALL BOYS ARE STRANGE!** I did notice Tyler talking to Josh though.

At least SOMEONE isn't afraid to talk to J.H. ☹

I sat beside Sophie and tried to concentrate on the pastor's message. Unfortunately, all I could think about was the school dance, Josh, and if I was even going.

I had a better chance of jetting to Paris for Fashion Week than getting asked to that dance!!!! Even though it was a few days since the broccoli disaster, I still couldn't speak another word to Josh.

But when our pastor began talking about Esther, he really got my attention. I couldn't help but wonder how on earth she had the nerve to go before the king and plead for her people's lives. Now THAT took some bravery! Maybe I could just brave it and walk right up to Josh at his locker on Monday . . .

OR NOT. If I said something dumb, Miranda Maroni would no doubt be standing there to **LAUGH HER HEAD OFF.** ☹

I tried to block it out of my mind and really think more about Esther. Being the fashion designer that I am, I couldn't help but wonder what kind of dress Esther wore at the banquet. I'm sure it was GORGEOUS!

I even googled "clothes in Bible times" when I got home. I kinda wish I could have lived back then. The royal clothes were SO ELEGANT, and the rings, bracelets, and earrings were BEAUTIFUL!

MONDAY, MARCH 29

Tyler enrolled at my school today. I can't imagine starting at a new school and having to meet all kinds of new people. That's gotta be tough. Of course, as soon as Tyler set foot into the building, Miranda had to make SURE that Tyler saw HER. AND she had to make sure that Josh saw her talking to Tyler.

That girl is **BOY CRAZY.** ☹ Why can't boys figure her out already? Tyler was totally clueless about the whole thing.

I tried to ignore her and instead gave Tyler the DL about our teachers. I'd want someone to do the same for me if it were the other way around. Naturally, I warned him about Mr. Finkleman. On the other hand, I promised that he'd love Mrs. Gibson. ☺

That was easy. If I don't become a world famous fashion designer, maybe I'll teach art—just like her. She not only lets us create art with any medium (like clay, paint, pencil, pastels, whatever), but we also get to come up with our OWN ideas instead of being told what to draw.

   She's nothing like our old art teacher,
Mrs. Francis, who made every kid draw
the same picture of a cat, over and over
and over. By the end of the year, I could draw that goofy
cat with my eyes closed!
   If you ask me, Mrs. Francis didn't know the meaning of
art! There's more to drawing than being a copy "cat."
   LOLOLOLOLOL!!!!

BO-RING!

Today Mrs. Gibson made a SHOCKING ANNOUNCEMENT on the intercom: "Don't forget, the big Middle School Art Show will be held on the first Monday after the dance. That's just three weeks away."

Oh, no! This is the worst thing ever!

I have to get my entry ready ASAP!!! Forget about the dance that no one has asked me to.

NO PRESSURE, RIGHT???

I didn't have any time to waste and went to Mrs. Gibson's room at break. I decided to show her the TRÈS CHIC dress sketch I've been working on and get her opinion. I pointed out the off-the-shoulder look, the details along the hemline, and that I planned on coloring it black. (The most chic of all the fashion colors, of course!) And guess what?

SHE LOVED IT!!!

She also asked me why I wasn't turning in a REAL dress. How did she KNOW???

There are only a few people who know I design clothes to ACTUALLY WEAR, and Mrs. Gibson is one of them. But how did she guess I'd already started cutting out some of the black fabric, just for fun?

I'd only had the nerve to carry one of my purses to school and wear one of the belts I'd made. There was NO WAY I could wear a homemade dress as long as Miranda Maroni was in the building.

Then Mrs. Gibson reminded me that artists have to be proud of their creations. "Even van Gogh had to be willing to let other people see his work," she said. "I just know you're going to wow me with your entry!"

Mrs. Gibson did have a point about needing to be proud of my work. I need to check out van Gogh's stuff online.

NOTE TO SELF:
GOOGLE VAN GOGH ON
THE COMPUTER TONIGHT.

Super
Star!

I could NOT concentrate for a SINGLE MINUTE when I went on to Mr. Finkleman's science class. Instead of filling out the worksheet on atoms, I zoned out and wrote in my diary:

Four Reasons Why I Should Talk to Josh

1. He is the cutest boy in class.
2. I notice him pray before lunch, which is totally cool.
3. He might even help me with my MATH—which I STINK AT!
4. I MUST go to the spring dance or be EMBARRASSED FOR LIFE!

Three Reasons Why I Should NOT Talk to Josh

1. He probably wouldn't even speak to me anyway, due to the broccoli humiliation.
2. Besides being smart in math, he's also the captain of the basketball team. He probably thinks art kids are WEIRD.
3. He actually SPEAKS to Miranda, so obviously there is something very wrong with him!

Then I got busted. Mr. Finkleman saw what I was doing and gave me "the look."

I FELT HORRIBLE. ☹

Luckily, he didn't send me to detention! But now Finkleman was upset with me, AND Mrs. Gibson was expecting me to WOW her with my art entry.

AGAIN—NO PRESSURE!!!!!!!!!!

This put me in a bad mood for the rest of the day. And to make matters worse, it happened to be a S.A.D. night at home.

I do NOT feel like sitting at the dinner table and thinking up something good to say about my day. But I have no choice. . . .

MOM'S GOOD DAY FACT:

Every kid was well behaved at the dentist's office today, and not a single kid had a cavity. She also said that she could take me dress shopping on Friday. YES!!!!!!!!!!!!!!!!!!

DAD'S GOOD DAY FACT: He received a letter from Spirit Ministries, and they can't wait to see all of us soon.

(The only way I'm going on a road trip is if Rosey stays at home or in another galaxy!)

MY GOOD DAY FACT: TOTAL BLANK.

I thought and thought and thought. I finally mentioned, "Mrs. Gibson really likes my idea for the art contest. That's about it for me."

THE GERM'S GOOD DAY FACT: Rosey has now learned to sit on command, roll over, and use the toilet in the bathroom.

OUR bathroom?????

GRRROOOOSSS!!!!!!!!!!

I will NEVER EVER use that bathroom again—EVER!

To keep from strangling the Germ, I decided to get on the computer and google: Vincent van Gogh. ANYTHING to quit thinking about a skunk sitting on my toilet!

After looking at a few of the images, I could see why Mrs. Gibson liked van Gogh's paintings. Every single painting is colorful, bright, and swirly. I think my favorite is his self-portrait, even though he looks sort of sad. The website said the only person who wanted to buy van Gogh's art was his brother, Theo, who felt sorry for him. Everyone else made fun of him. Van Gogh died before ever knowing how popular his work would become. Some of his paintings are now worth MILLIONS of dollars.

I know how van Gogh must have felt. When I overhead Miranda making fun of my drawings, it really hurt. At least I have Sophie to lean on, just like van Gogh had his brother. Thankfully, ALL of us have Jesus to lean on, no matter what! On some days, it seems like He's the only one who understands. . . .

ADD TO PRAYER LIST: Thank God that He's always there for me and understands my feelings.

TUESDAY, MARCH 30

ANOTHER T.T.
(Better known as Terrible Tuesday)

I didn't do it today.

I tried.

But. I. Could. Not. Speak. To. Josh. ☹ ☹ ☹ ☹

I thought about it at our lockers since his is only a few down from mine. But all I could do was THINK about it. Josh was talking to Tyler, so it should have been easy. Tyler always says, "Hey, Catie" in the hallway, so I KNOW at least one of them would say something.

BUT I FROZE
.... AGAIN.

What is wrong with me???

Obviously there's nothing wrong with Miranda Maroni. She and Emily waltzed right up to Josh and Tyler and talked to them like it was the easiest thing ever!

"Hey Josh! Very cool shirt you have on," Miranda said, smiling like some weird model in a toothpaste commercial. (I could even see her batting her eyelashes all the way from where I was standing!)

Emily was being nice too.
"It's nice to meet you Tyler. If you need help with finding any of your classes, just ask. I hope you really like it here."
And to make matters worse, both Tyler AND Josh smiled and actually TALKED to them!

That Miranda! She. Is. Boy. Crazy. And she makes it look like fun. I just wish she'd leave Josh alone.
I just wish . . . I wish I could talk to boys like she does. ☹

I couldn't wait until school was over. I went home, grabbed a snack, went up to my room, and hid for the rest of the evening.

I tried to forget all about the locker drama and brainstormed on my art project, the très chic dress sketch. I even got the fabric out and sewed together a couple of pieces just to see how it looked. Then I went back to my sketch.

I kept remembering what Mrs. Gibson said about being confident in my work. Still, I wasn't so sure. . . .

I might even talk to Mom about it. She has pretty good taste . . . for a mom. She even surprised me by picking up some new pastel pencils on her way home from work. I'm not sure what's gotten into her, but I'm not going to complain.

MAYBE I SHOULD !!! ASK FOR THAT NEW CELL PHONE??? !!!

I could hardly wait for Friday to get here! I love looking at fashion—and I was dying to find the perfect dress for the dance. I hope, hope, HOPE someone (Josh???) asks me. But the way my luck was going, I would be tagging along with Sophie. Which would be MORTIFYING. ☹ ☹ ☹

Sophie messaged me on my computer this evening, trying to cheer me up:

Sophie: Catie, CHILL. I'm sure you'll be at that dance. Seriously, you're freaking out over nothing.

Me: Easy for U to say. At least u know who will ask U.... Everyone knows Matt Hutchinson has a crush on U.

Sophie: Well, he hasn't asked me yet. lol.

Me: I know he will. PRAY THAT JOSH ASKS ME!!! I SOOO want to go to the dance with him!!!

Sophie: Just quit thinking about it. Go sketch some of your fashions or something. Ttyl. Oh, and I have a plan for school 2morrow. Stay tuned. ☺

I can hardly wait to go shopping with Mom.

I already know what color dress I want: TURQUOISE. It's one of my favorite colors. Maybe with silver sequins and silver earrings? And I'm sure I can find some silver heels at the mall with just a touch of bling. CUTEEEEEE!

Oh how I wish Friday would hurry and get here!!!!!!!!!!

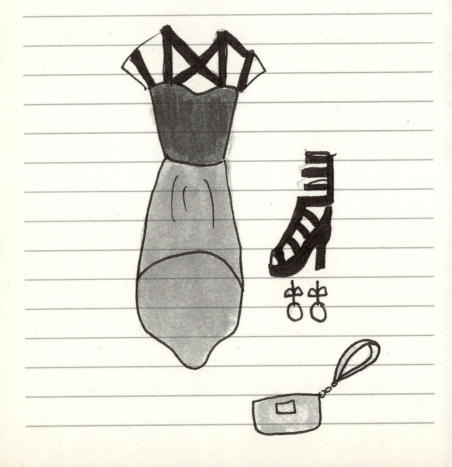

But I might as well wear a paper bag over my head if no one asks me to the dance.

I don't know WHY I'm even THINKING about a dress! I'm almost positive I'll be stuck at home with the Germ . . . and Rosey. ☹

THIS CANNOT HAPPEN. I REPEAT: THIS CANNOT HAPPEN!!!!

Add to Prayer List: Trust in God to work everything out. He promises that, after all!

WEDNESDAY, MARCH 31

Today was supposed to have been THE DAY.
BUT IT WAS **NOT**.
BLAME IT ON THE HAMBURGER!!!!!!

Sophie and I were sitting at our usual table in the cafeteria and discussing her PLAN, OPERATION: SPRING DANCE. (Looking back on it, I wondered what had been going on in that brain of hers!!!)

OPERATION: SPRING DANCE

Josh and the rest of the basketball team always sat together. They were usually the first ones to inhale their food and had even invited Tyler to sit with them.

I didn't have much time to put our plan into action, and it was just my luck that we had hamburgers for lunch. UGH!

We had two HUGE choices: a hamburger with cheese or a hamburger without cheese. Yeah, big selection. We had to go to the salad bar if we wanted anything else. THAT'S WHERE MY PLAN WAS SUPPOSED TO GO INTO ACTION.

I repeat: WAS SUPPOSED TO. . . .

So this is how it all went down. . . .

Sophie: Okay, Catie, so when you see Josh going up to the salad bar to squirt ketchup on his burger, you go up there and put mustard on yours at the same time.

Me: But I don't even LIKE mustard on my burger!

Sophie: Do you want a date to the dance or not?

Me: Okay, okay . . . good grief!

Sophie: Just say something like, "Hey, Josh. How's it going?" Then wait and see what he says.

Me: THEN what do I say?

Sophie: How should I know? You can handle it from there.

Me: This has to be the dumbest idea ever, but okay. Wish me luck.

Josh went up to the salad bar just like we'd planned. After a sharp elbow in the side from Sophie, I walked up to the salad bar too. Josh had on the coolest blue T-shirt ever, and he even looked at me and SMILED!

He SMILED!!!

Then I did something **TOTALLY DUMB**: I noticed that I'd forgotten to bring my hamburger with me to the salad bar! What was I thinking? My mind went blank, and I couldn't help but look over at Sophie. Luckily she mouthed the words and reminded me what to say.

"Uh, how's it going, Josh?" I asked quickly. I suddenly felt dizzy and stuck out my arm to lean onto the salad bar.

Fainting was NOT an option.

Just as Josh was opening his mouth to say, *"Hi Catie, how's—"* **THE DISASTER HAPPENED.**

I had accidentally leaned over onto the mustard pump and—

KA—WHAM!!!!!!!!!

Mustard squirted ALL OVER Josh's shirt! IT WAS RUINED! He looked like a human hotdog. Everyone in the entire cafeteria saw it and CRACKED UP. I WANTED TO CRAWL UNDER THE TABLE AND HIDE!

"Oh, I'm SO SORRY, Josh!" I think I might have raised my voice. "I'm really REALLY sorry!" I grabbed as many napkins as I could from the dispenser and tried to help him wipe the mustard off. But the more I tried, the worse it got.

IT WAS A NIGHTMARE!!!!!!!!!!

"No big deal," Josh mumbled and then bolted toward the bathroom. He even almost wiped out on a giant blob of mustard on the floor. THIS COULD NOT BE HAPPENING. ☹ ☹ ☹ Maybe this was a bad dream and I'd wake up from it later? It was like everything was going on in SLLLOOOW MOOOOTION. . . .

That's when Miranda had to come by and put her two cents in. She was the LAST girl on Earth I wanted to see. "Way to go, Catie," Miranda said. "Maybe you can serve hotdogs at the next basketball game. You sure know how to use the mustard pump!"

UGH!!!!!!!!!!!!!!!

It took more strength than Samson to hold my tongue and just walk away.

MY FIRST YEAR OF MIDDLE SCHOOL COULDN'T GET ANY WORSE!!

Maybe I could talk Mom and Dad into letting me switch schools. But what school would even want me? Embarrassing junk like this travels fast. I'm sure every kid in middle school has texted about it all over town.

As soon as I got home, I went straight to my room and cried . . . and prayed . . . **A LOT**. Dad was home and could tell that I was upset. It's SO HARD explaining stuff like this to my parents.

Me: Dad, today was **the worst day I've ever had in my entire life!** I'm serious. It was horrible. I really think I need to switch schools.

Dad: Whoa, hold on a second, Catie. Perhaps you should start from the beginning. Now slowly tell me what happened. It can't be as bad as you're saying.

Me: To start with, in a few weeks, we're having the goofiest dance ever at school. Some of the girls are going to the dance with guys. But I don't even know if I'm going! Nobody's asked me to go.

Dad: Why don't you just go with your friends and have fun? Is that what this is all about?

Me: Yes! I was HOPING Josh Henderson would ask me to go with him. But NO, I had to squirt mustard all over him in the cafeteria today! My life is ruined.

Dad: Josh Henderson from church? I'm sure he's already forgiven you, honey. I can tell this dance is important to you, but your life isn't ruined. I think the best thing to do is pray about it. Take this to God, and then trust that He'll handle it.

Me: Oh, okay . . .
whatever, Dad. Thanks.

I know Dad was trying to make me feel better, but some-times he just doesn't get it. I did take his advice, though, and read Jeremiah 32:27:

"I am the LORD,
the God of all mankind.
Is anything too hard for me?"

I have no choice but to have faith and hang on to God's Word. Hopefully everyone won't look at me tomorrow and run for cover. ☹

At least Sophie will be at school tomorrow, and we can analyze what went wrong. She's the one who came up with the whole OPERATION: SPRING DANCE thing in the first place! But it's not like Sophie forced me to do it.

Why do I always fall for every crazy thing???

I decided to work on my très chic dress sketch. I might even sew the MULTICOLORED sequins on the top of the REAL dress I was working on. I had to do SOMETHING to get my mind off things! But it was a LOT harder than I'd thought. I first used a tiny bit of fabric GLUE to PLACE the sequins on the fabric and then sewed them on by hand. It FELT LIKE I was working on a MOSAIC ALL over again. LUCKILY I had some experience with tweezers!

APRIL 1—APRIL FOOLS' DAY
... UGHHHHH ☹ ☹ ☹

How perfectly convenient it is that today is April Fools' Day! I feel like the BIGGEST JOKE EVER. I can only imagine what it's going to be like at school today. ☹ ☹ ☹

I'm so upset that I'm writing in my diary before school. Yeah, it's THAT BAD.

I begged Mom and Dad to let me stay home for a few days until this mustard mistake blows over. But of course they said the usual: "These things build character, Catie. If they're your real friends, they won't think twice about that silly mustard incident."

YEAH, RIGHT.

There's NO WAY I can get near Josh or his friends today, and I CERTAINLY can't show my face in the cafeteria for the next twenty years. Maybe I'LL just PUT a few granoLa bars in my backpack. If I'm Lucky, Mrs. Gibson might Let me hang out in the art room instead of going to Lunch.

I think I'LL try and bLock it out by doing a few sketches before school.

WELL, THAT DIDN'T WORK.

Whenever I draw anything, it usually ends up being an outfit—which is usually a dress. THEN I think of the school dance, and THEN I get upset all over again. NOT GOOD. Time to remember **JEREMIAH 32:27.** ☺

I'm gonna be late for school, so TTYL!!!!!

I was RIGHT, and my parents were WRONG. I couldn't WAIT to get home and write about it. My so-called friends did NOT forget about the "mustard incident."

Matt Hutchinson taped a sign to my back that said "I ♡ MUSTARD." I walked all the way to my locker on the other side of the building looking like a total loser. It was all I could do to remember what Dad had reminded me last night—to just let God handle it.

IT WAS HARD.

Luckily, Sophie found the sign on my back and threw it into the trash. Matt was probably just trying to show off in front of Sophie. I KNOW he has a crush on her.

At least that's what I overhead him tell Tyler. But if Matt thinks that putting a sign on my back is a way to look cool in front of Sophie, then he is TOTALLY WRONG. On top of everything else, Sophie is the principal's kid! What was he thinking?

Sophie let him have it. "Please don't do that, Matt. It's not very funny," she said. "In fact, it's terrible! You owe Catie an apology!"

I'm soooooooo lucky to have a friend like Sophie! I'd do the same thing for her if anyone taped something dumb to her back.

It seemed like everyone thought that they had to be the class comedian on April Fools' Day.

Five minutes before math class, Emily told Miranda we were having a ginormous test. She even said whoever failed it would have to do 95 math problems for homework. LOLOLOLOL. Miranda totally freaked! (I'll have to admit it was hilarious.) But then Emily felt bad and told Miranda that it was just a joke. SHEESH!

But the WORST prank happened to Josh.

SOMEONE put a can of sardines in his locker this morning. By the time our class made it over to that part of the building, the entire hallway REEKED!

It smelled so bad that I got sick to my stomach. But the boys in our class cracked up. "Hey, Josh, did you wear your deodorant today?" they asked. Or "Hey, Josh, since you loved mustard yesterday, maybe you need some tartar sauce now! You do smell sort of fishy!" They all bent over, laughing their heads off.

But Josh didn't.

I could tell that he wasn't happy about it. Of course, he tried to act cool and laugh right along with them, but I could tell that he was upset. From drowning in mustard yesterday to having a locker that STUNK today, Josh has the worst luck ever. Even worse than ME!

But then I don't know what happened—without even thinking twice about it, I went over and SPOKE TO JOSH. Yes, that's what I said. I simply walked over and started talking! After all, he is my friend, and I felt sorry for him. God must have given me strength and heard my prayers this morning!

Me: Hey, Josh, sorry about what they did to your locker. That totally STINKS. . . . Oh, what I MEANT to say was it wasn't very nice. (Why did I use the word stink—what was I thinking!)

Josh: *Oh, it's no big deal. I don't know why people want to do stuff that's so dumb. It wasn't even funny.*

Me: *You got that right! Some of our friends act like total first graders. I'm sorry about yesterday. You know, about the whole mustard thing. . . .*

Josh: *No prob, Catie. No big deal . . . it was an old shirt anyway.*

Our little talk was awesome! I actually felt like a NORMAL person having a NORMAL conversation with a friend!

I WENT HOME IN THE BEST MOOD OF ALL TIME!

And of course, SINCE it is April Fools' Day, and SINCE the Germ is such an easy target, I couldn't resist playing a harmless joke. While he was in front of the TV watching one of his goofy animal shows, I tiptoed ever so quietly into his bedroom and picked up Rosey. I quickly rushed to my bedroom, hid her in my closet, and closed the door.

Actually, I put Rosey in a box and then put her in my closet—just in case she decided to go wild and eat the buttons off a sweater or something. I never trust that ticking stink bomb.

I then flopped down onto the couch and put my plan into action. . . .

Me: Hey, Germ, what's up with you? I think this is the first time I've ever seen you watch TV without that rotten creature.

Germ: Whatever, Catie. For your information, Rosey likes to rest this time of the day. Even skunks need some time to relax.

Me: Whatever. But I walked by your room just now, and I didn't see her.

My brother immediately jumped up from the sofa and ran to his room—just long enough for me to grab the remote and put it on the Fashion Channel. ☺

He suddenly flew back into the living room looking like he was about to faint. "SOMEONE HAS STOLEN ROSEY! CALL 9-1-1! SHE'S DISAPPEARED! SHE'S PROBABLY BEEN SKUNK-NAPPED BY A PET STORE! THEY'LL FEED HER NOTHING BUT HAMSTER FOOD!" he screamed at the top of his lungs.

LOLOLOLOL!!!! This was the best April Fools' joke in the history of April Fools' jokes! I had to cover my face with a pillow so the Germ wouldn't see me crack up.

But then the Germ totally blew it. He called Mom at work and cried like a big baby. I had no choice but to grab the phone and explain to her that it was just a little joke. Luckily Mom understood and didn't get too upset. She did remind me of the golden rule, though, and that I should tell the Germ that I was sorry. SHEESH! He was SUCH a big baby!

I couldn't help but think about the pranks pulled on Josh today though. I guess I should have thought about that BEFORE I hid Rosey in the closet!

FRIDAY, APRIL 2

SHOPPPINGGGGG DAYYYYYY!!!!!!

I couldn't wait to write in my diary about
what an AWESOME day it's been!

Even though I still wondered if I'd even
go to the dance, what girl EVER turns
down a trip to the mall?

I even broke down and told Mom all
about the drama at school: about Mr.
Martin's thoughts about ladies and gentlemen,
about Miranda being a typical pain, and even about me
speaking to Josh after the sardine nightmare.

Of course, Mom went on and on. "Catie, it's
not the end of the world if you don't go to
that dance with Josh. You can go with Sophie.
And maybe Miranda isn't as bad as you think.
Just be patient."

UGH.

WHO COULD BE PATIENT
AT A TIME LIKE THIS??

We finally made it to the mall, and I could hardly wait to start looking. ☺ First we went to Fashion Frenzy. ZERO LUCK.

Most of the dresses were so short that Mom instantly said, "NO WAY." Some looked tiny enough to fit an eight-year-old. ☹ Anyway, we have a dress code rule that says a dress can't be more than three inches above the knee.

But some of the girls in my class SOOOO IGNORE that rule. When they sit down, you can almost see everything . . . and I do mean everything.

Talk about a FASHION DISASTER!!! But, of course, they get all KINDS of looks from some of the guys. ☹

I don't want attention THAT bad and from THOSE kind of boys. ☹ Mom says the boys will change their ways one of these days, but who knows.

NOT!

166

I'd MUCH rather be decent and fashionable all at the same time. ☺ But I don't want clothes that look like something my great-grandmother would wear either. That would be just WEIRD.

Even though I didn't find anything at Fashion Frenzy, Mom urged me to keep looking.

THEN.

I.

HIT.

THE.

JACKPOT!!!!!!!!!!

We went to my all-time favorite store: Unique Boutique.

LOVE!!! LOVE!!! LOVE!!!

FIVE REASONS WHY UNIQUE BOUTIQUE IS THE COOLEST STORE EVER:

1. Girls that look like fashion models shop here.
2. They have accessories to match ANY and EVERY kind of outfit.
3. It always smells good in the store. (Dad says it's some kind of sales gimmick, but who cares! It's better than smelling like Rosey!)
4. It's FASHION HEAVEN! Everything in the store is color coordinated. Pink dresses, pink shoes, pink jewelry. Turquoise dresses, turquoise hair bands, turquoise every—thing. You get the picture. ☺
5. THEY CARRY CLAIRE HUNTER DESIGNS!!!!!!!!!!!!!!!

After looking for only a few minutes, I FINALLY FOUND IT:

The MOST BEAUTIFUL DRESS in THE UNIVERSE!!!!!!!!!!!

WHOA!

$$$

It's the PERFECT length, the PERFECT color, the PERFECT BRAND, the PERFECT EVERYTHING!!!!!

But it was also very expensive, since it was the Claire Hunter brand.

"The only way I can afford this is if you put in some of your own money, Catie," Mom said. "You're going to have to make a choice. I know you're saving up for a cell phone, but if you want this dress, you're gonna have to pitch in."

I didn't think twice about my decision and agreed that I'd give Mom part of my savings. She then put it on layaway and told the sales lady she'd pick it up when she got paid next week.

YES!!! YES!!! YES!!
I AM GOING TO BE THE PROUD OWNER
OF A CLAIRE HUNTER DRESS!!!!

I hoped it was returnable though. After all, if no one asks me to the dance, I don't need the most GORGEOUS DRESS in the history of gorgeous dresses. I've decided that if no one asks me to the dance, then I'm not going anyway. ☹

Hopefully I won't have to worry about it since I'm praying that Josh asks me to the dance!

Our last stop on the way home was the craft store. Unfortunately, I knew it was because of the Germ, who was working on a house for Rosey. Yes, that's what I said.

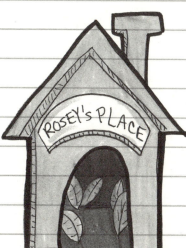

The Germ has finally gone over the edge. He has paint, fake plants, and craft junk all over his room. He even used a red crayon and wrote "Rosey's Place" on the cardboard roof.

Seriously . . . **THE GERM HAS LOST IT.**

He's been decorating the crazy thing for weeks and is always asking Mom to pick up stuff. "Rosey needs a home that looks like her natural habitat!" he'd say over and over. "Skunks are very territorial, according to the animal channel, and so we need to make her feel as comfortable as possible."

If he REALLY wanted to put it in its natural habitat, he'd kick it out of the house and send it on its way— SOMEWHERE ELSE!

But when we went to the Hobby House this time, Mom didn't go to the artificial plant section. We went to the sewing section. Maybe she was gonna let me pick out a few yards of fabric. I was getting a little low.

But when Mom loaded a BRAND NEW Singer sewing machine into the shopping cart, I almost passed out!!! I assumed that she was getting herself one since I constantly use hers.

"I know I work a LOT," she said, "and I wish I didn't have to. But sometimes I have to work so that I can provide extra things for you and your brother. And today, I want to buy you something that I think you'LL reaLLy use. It has aLL kinds of new stitch choices, and it's a far cry from MY oLd machine. This one should be MORE reLiabLe and not tear up as easiLy."

I. WAS. SPEECHLESS.

I couLd hardLy wait to caLL Sophie!!!!

"It might take a while to figure out every knob on this new machine, but we will. Technology sure has changed!" Mom said. "You're very creative, Catherine. I think it's about time you even wear one of your creations to school. They're good enough, you know."

Is this how the big New York designers got started? Maybe their moms taught them how to sew too? I'd have to google that for sure!

So tonight I'm not going to think about that dumb dance! I have more important things to do:

1. Call Sophie and tell her everything!

2. Get out my sketchbook and design more CATIE CONRAD ORIGINALS!

ADD TO PRAYER LIST:
Thank God for having a Mom that understands how much I LOVE TO DESIGN FASHIONS!

SATURDAY, APRIL 3

My luck was starting to turn around. Having two days in a row that were drama free was NICE!

I can hardly believe it myself, but Mom and I figured out how to use EVERY knob on my new sewing machine. I also had a new shirt design to try. I figure if I'm ever going to have the nerve to wear one of my designs to school, I'd rather start out small with just a simple shirt.

Some pink fabric from the Hobby House was the PERFECT choice. I even found some cool buttons from the old craft box in the closet. Just as soon as I'd laid out the pieces, I could hardly wait to stitch the whole thing together using one of the new stitch settings. Of course, Mom made me practice sewing on old fabric scraps first.

I didn't know that a sewing machine could zoom so fast! Mom's old machine is pokey compared to this one. My lines were a little wavy in the beginning, but soon I sewed like a pro!

G.G.

My new shirt design ended up being WAY more amazing than I'd thought! It might not show up on a runway anytime soon, but at least it's a step in the right direction. ☺

I can hardly wait to do two things:

1. TRY ON MY SHIRT with my favorite jeans. Mom said it should fit fine, but I'm not so sure. One arm sleeve is a little longer than the other, but . . . I can always roll up the one weird sleeve. Maybe I'll start a new fashion trend. ☺

2. I can't wait to TAKE A PIC and e-mail it to Sophie. She will FREAK and want one just like it!

GTG!!!!!

I was right, Sophie freaked.

I mean, TOTALLY freaked! She loved my shirt (which, BTW, fit perfectly) and said it was the most beautiful shirt she'd ever seen. She probably only said that because she's my best friend, but it was still nice. She also said she wants one exactly like it. (Told ya! I know her like a book!)

Since it was Saturday and since my room looked semi-decent, Mom said Sophie could come over and hang out.

I HAVE THE MOST
AWESOME DAY PLANNED:

First, I'll design a shirt for Sophie and get her thoughts on it. A designer HAS to please the customer, after all. ☺ I'm a little nervous about sewing in front of Sophie, but I don't know why. She's seen me squirt mustard on Josh, has taken dumb notes off my back, and was the ONLY one to point out the green junk between my teeth! Why should I be nervous in front of my BFF?

After we make her shirt (fingers crossed that it will fit!), I'm thinking we could stir up a few facial creams? Or body lotions? I'll wait and see what Sophie thinks about it since she's the pro on that kind of stuff.

Sophie came over, and we were having the BEST day ever. She brought over a few yards of sparkly blue fabric and could hardly wait to see me in action!

I took my time cutting out the pieces and double-checked everything with Mom. After an hour or two of HARD WORK at the sewing machine, it was finally finished! Sophie actually squealed out loud when she tried it on, and it fit perfectly. We took a zillion pics of it with her iPhone. (In my opinion, it looked as cool as the shirts at Unique Boutique AND was a whole lot cheaper. ☺)

THEN A DISASTER HAPPENED . . .

Sophie found a cool recipe for a face scrub that promised to make our skin "as soft as a baby" and "oil free." That sounded great since my skin is always like a grease pit. ☹

Sophie usually knows what she's doing, but these ingredients sounded GROSS. Especially mixed together!

Perfectly Sweet Facial Scrub (NOT!!!)

5 teaspoons of water

3 teaspoons of plain yogurt

2 teaspoons of honey

3 teaspoons of coffee grounds

I should have known better than to think this could actually work. ☹ I didn't even like to DRINK coffee, so rubbing coffee grounds on my face sounded INSANE!

We put on our bathrobes (you MUST wear a robe for the real spa effect), pulled our hair back with headbands, and rubbed the coffee goop all over our faces. We looked like we'd done a face plant into a Starbucks trashcan. At least we scared Rosey and the Germ to pieces when we hid behind his bedroom door wearing the face goop. LOLOLOL!!!!

IT WAS PRICELESS.

But when Sophie said we had to leave the stuff on our faces for ten minutes, THAT'S WHEN THE TROUBLE STARTED.

After only five minutes wearing that goop, my skin started feeing a little itchy. And then A LOT ITCHY. So did Sophie's. We couldn't stand it any longer and rushed to the bathroom to wash it off of our faces as quickly as possible. Then I looked into the mirror . . .

AND FREAKED!!!!!

A bright pink rash covered my entire face—especially around my eyes. And Sophie's face looked even worse than mine.

IT WAS AWFUL! IT WAS GROSS!
I looked like I had DIAPER RASH ON THE WRONG END!

We had no choice but to show Mom. She quickly went to the medicine cabinet and rubbed some type of ointment onto our skin that was supposed to help with the redness. NOT. Sophie went home looking like a medical experiment gone bad.

What started out as a perfectly good day ENDED AS THE WORST DAY EVER.

Just ONCE I wish things could go MY WAY! But Mom reminds me that God allows us to go through bad stuff to make us stronger in our faith. I DON'T HAVE A CLUE why God allowed this CRAZY rash on my CRAZY face, but I have to trust HIM!

ADD TO PRAYER LIST:
Pray that this RASH goes away
by Monday!!!

Faith.

SUNDAY, APRIL 4

I had no choice but to wear sunglasses to church today. It took me over an hour to get Mom and Dad's permission to wear them, but they eventually caved. Sophie had to do the exact same thing with her parents. Anyway, we looked WAY scarier without the sunglasses, since we still had this freak face rash.

We got lots of stares when we walked into the chapel but tried to ignore them. I hate admitting it, but I hoped that Josh would NOT be at church today. He was the LAST person I wanted to run into looking like this.

BUT NO SUCH LUCK.

Josh did a double take when he saw us walk in. I also noticed him whispering something to Tyler, which I'm SURE was something about how weird we looked.

At least Tyler came up to me and seemed nice.

"Hi, Catie. Are you okay? Is anything wrong?"

Maybe Josh put him up to asking me?

"I'm fine, Tyler," I said. "Why wouldn't I be?"

Even though I was wearing sunglasses, I CLEARLY saw Tyler look at Josh and roll his eyes.

Oh, but if MIRANDA MARONI would have been at church wearing sunglasses, Josh and Tyler would have thought she was the COOLEST girl around. They wouldn't ask if SHE was okay. They'd just think she wore sunglasses because she was so cool. ☹ ☹

UGH! I DO NOT UNDERSTAND GUYS!!!

My face had better CLEAR UP SOON because the dance is right around the corner! Of course, there's STILL that SMALL PROBLEM of no one asking ME yet. . . . ☹ ☹ ☹

More LATER . . . GTG!!!

Tonight was S.A.D. night, and Dad had MORE news about the MISSION trip. Even though I was excited to be going, I wished Dad understood why this WHOLE thing was BAD TIMING.

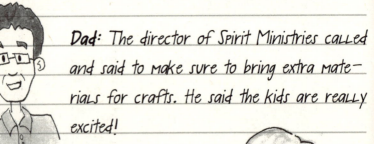

Dad: The director of Spirit Ministries called and said to MAKE sure to bring extra materials for crafts. He said the kids are really excited!

Mom: That IS good news. This is going to be one awesome trip! Dr. Hamilton even donated a box of kids' toothbrushes to bring along.

Me: Dad, is there any way possible that you could change the date for this trip? I really have important plans and stuff.

Germ: You don't have any plans! Especially if you're talking about that dumb dance! No one has even asked you! Who wants to go with a MONSTER FACE? That's my good thing for today—Catie is a monster face.

Me: One more word, and I won't be hiding Rosey as a prank—I'll hide that stink bomb for LIFE! Now that's something GREAT!

Dad: Okay, okay, that's enough, you two. The dance isn't until the week AFTER we get back, Catie. So you have plenty of time to prepare. Remember what we discussed. There will be other dances, and it's important that we serve God.

I cannot beLieve that I'm being forced to go to Arizona this week! Even though I'm excited to hang out on a rez, I MUST have my ceLL phone—just in case someone caLLs and asks ME TO THE DANCE!

But my STONE AGE phone probabLy doesn't even WORK in the southwest! ? ? ?

Me: Okay, so you're not going to believe this. We are leaving THIS WEEK for Arizona. And by this week, I mean TUESDAY—as in DAY AFTER TOMORROW!

Sophie: Cool! I'd love to visit Arizona. I'm sure there's not a single girl in our class who has ever been to a reservation. Not even Miranda! ☺

Me: SOPH! Can't you see that I need to be HERE? We still have to make "Operation Spring Dance" a success. Know what I mean?

Sophie: Don't worry about it! This dance is making you CRAZY! Who knows, maybe you and the GERM may actually have fun on this trip. ☺ Oh, and FYI, I told your mother I'd feed Rosey while you guys are gone.

Me: YUCK! Have you MET my brother? He's

HORRIBLE. And that skunk stinks!

Sophie: LOL! It's OK.

Me: C U at school tomorrow. Remember, we're wearing

our new shirts. ☺

Sophie: I remember. I am SO pumped! C YA!

Why did I say that about my brother? That was dumb!
Even though he could be a total pain, he wasn't horrible.
Well, not usually. But I can't think about that now. I have
a TON of work to do on my fashion sketch! I might even use
my new machine to finish and hem the real dress.

⑤ Prayer List

Ask God to forgive me
for saying that the
Germ is horrible.

MONDAY, APRIL 5

WHAT IS WRONG WITH ME?

I've been up since 6:00 AM! I've also been writing in this crazy diary, as you can tell. CCCRRRAAAAZZZYYYY.

I'm so nervous about wearing my new shirt to school today. I even asked Mom to iron it—TWICE!

What if everyone thinks it's hideous? And since Soph is wearing hers, too, we'll probably BOTH be called HIDEOUS!

I've decided to wear both sleeves rolled up, just to play it safe, along with my silver earrings and faded jeans. I might even wear a little strawberry lip gloss and ask Mom to braid my hair. YES!

GTG GET READY!!!!

Sophie beat me to school and was pacing back and forth in front of my locker. She looked AWESOME in her new shirt! She also wore blue dangle earrings, a black skirt, and tall boots.

I couldn't believe it: my best friend was wearing a CATIE CONRAD ORIGINAL . . . AND SO WAS I!

But we both were nervous.

Miranda Maroni hadn't made it to school yet. She would definitely have something RUDE to say! ☹

WORRIED Me: Has anyone laughed yet? I'll probably start sweating and get armpit stains. I'll DIE if that happens!

CALM Sophie: Will you just CHILL OUT for a second? You're acting all crazy again.

NERVOUS Me: I'm sure Miranda will fall in the floor laughing at a pit-stained shirt with one sleeve longer than the other. What was I thinking wearing this dumb shirt to school?

BEST FRIEND Sophie: I told you, no one will even notice it's a homemade shirt. And WHO CARES! I love my shirt! Catie, get a grip.

But JUST as the words left Sophie's mouth, I heard Miranda and Emily coming up the hall. They were talking about the dance . . . OF COURSE!

Emily: I still haven't found a dress yet, but Mom and I are going shopping tomorrow.

Miranda: I can hardly wait! I've got it narrowed between two dresses but can't decide which I like best.

Emily: Lucky you! I'm having the worst luck ever. Every dress is either too tight or ten sizes too big.

At least I was a few steps ahead of Miranda since I already had a dress. ☺ But of course, she was WAY ahead of me since boys were practically lining up to ask her to the dance. ☹

Suddenly, Emily spotted Sophie and me at our lockers. Of course, Miranda just stood there and stared at us from head to toe. I didn't even want to know what was going on in that brain of hers.

Emily: I like your shirt, Sophie—especially the buttons. Cool. (Of course, Emily didn't tell ME that, not in front of Miranda!)

Sophie: Thanks—I just got it yesterday. I love it too.

Emily: Did you get it at Unique Boutique? Love that store.

Sophie: Me too! I could stay in that store FOREVER. Oh, and nah, I didn't get it there.

Emily: What brand is it? Did you order it online or some-thing?

   (Why did Emily suddenly decide to be so chatty and ask so many questions?)

Sophie: No . . . uh . . . the brand is **C.C.O.** I think.

Me: Soph, we're late for class! We gotta go!

SOPHIE IS THE BEST!!!!

She can come up with a reply in TWO SECONDS. I would have NEVER thought to call the brand of our shirts **C.C.O.**—which I knew stood for Catie Conrad Original. ☺ No wonder she is the class brainiac!!!

   And I'm positive that Emily liked the shirt I had on too. I saw how she looked at it. I bet Miranda even liked my creations—she's just too Miranda to say something nice.

I still can't believe that Dad is making us leave for Arizona tomorrow.

TOMORROW!
WHAT WERE MY PARENTS THINKING?

Since the school dance is a few days after I get back, I need to get asked to it before I leave for Arizona—like TODAY!!!!

And the big art show is coming up too. **I HAVE DOUBLE THE STRESS!!!**

If I even have a CHANCE of winning, this has to be the BEST FASHION DRAWING OF ALL TIME!

IT HAS TO BE AS GOOD AS A VAN GOGH MASTERPIECE!!!!

Sophie messaged me on the computer as soon as we got home from school. Matt had texted her AND asked her to the dance!

I KNEW IT.

Sophie: Oh My Gosh. I cannot believe that Matt asked me. It's too weird. Should I go, just as good friends, of course?

Me: Duh. Sure you're going! Just let me know how it goes because I don't think I'll be there.

Sophie: You've still got one more day before you leave—right? Want me to ask Matt to ask Josh if he's going to ask you?

Me: Ummm . . . I don't know. Should you? I thought he would ask Miranda.

Sophie: I think she just talks a lot! Got to go!

Don't get me wrong, I'm glad Matt asked Sophie to the dance. He's a nice guy and all that. He'd even apologized to me for the whole April Fools' Day prank.

But I'll admit that I'm a little jealous. ☹ ☹ ☹

I kept checking my phone every ten minutes . . . and then every two minutes, hoping that Sophie would leave me a voicemail.

BUT. NO. SUCH. LUCK.

No messages. ☹
NOT FROM SOPHIE. ☹ ☹
NOT FROM JOSH. ☹ ☹ ☹

I decided to go to my room and do what I always do to get my mind off things: PRAY and work on my fashion designs. Maybe I'll enter an actual dress one of these days, but for now I was happy to just turn in my drawing. I hung up the real très chic dress in my closet and closed the door.

NOTE TO SELF:
QUIT ACTING LIKE A BABY,
EVEN THOUGH THIS WHOLE
DANCE THING IS TOTALLY
NERVE-RACKING!!!

TUESDAY, APRIL 6 (ARIZONA)

THIS. IS. IT.

We're leaving for our mission trip today.

I'm also turning in my entry for the school art contest. FINGERS CROSSED! Even though it's not the actual dress, it's the best drawing that I've ever done. I repeat—**EVER**. Maybe I'll have the nerve to enter a dress in the art show next year.

I still can't believe that I'm leaving for Arizona right after school today. TODAY OF ALL DAYS! ☹ Dad's timing could **NOT** be worse!

GTG, even though I'M TOTALLY NERVOUS about going to school today. ☹

UGH!!!!

I wish I'd NEVER gone to school today!!!!

T. T. T. T. T.
TOTALLY TERRIBLE TUESDAY TIMES TEN!!!!

Why is it that EVERY Tuesday of my life is TERRIBLE?

As soon as I got to school this morning, I noticed Tyler and Emily talking by the lockers. I'M SURE it was about the dance, but I didn't want to act nosy.

Just when I was about to say hi to them, Tyler quickly walked off and barely said hi. **What was with him?**

I was the one who introduced him to my friends at school and didn't make him feel like the new kid. I was the one who tried to warn him of what a PAIN the Germ was when they came over for dinner. I was the one who warned him about Mr. Finkleman's horrible quizzes!

SOME KIND OF FRIEND HE WAS!
WEIRD. WEIRD. WEIRD.

I told Sophie all about it as we walked to our first period class. That's when my best friend GAVE ME THE NEWS:

JOSH MESSAGED MIRANDA AND ASKED HER TO THE DANCE LAST NIGHT.

Josh told Tyler all about it, Tyler told Emily, and Emily told Sophie. ☹ ☹ ☹ ☹ ☹ ☹

I knew it might happen, but I still couldn't believe the boy I liked was asking . . . HER.

WHY MIRANDA MARONI??? WHY???

At least my best friend was the one to tell me instead of Miranda rubbing it in my face. I secretly hoped they'd have a horrible time.

(Prayer List—pray about not wishing the worst on anyone.)

But that was just the beginning . . .

Today was P.E.—my LEAST favorite subject!

And on top of everything, Coach Calloway had the brilliant idea to do a VOLLEYBALL SCRIMMAGE. Yes—Miranda's favorite sport.
WHY????

I STINK at volleyball and had been humiliated enough for one day.
Sophie reminded me that none of the other kids even knew that I'd wanted Josh Henderson to ask me to that dance.

BUT I KNEW IT, AND THAT WAS BAD ENOUGH.

But NOT bad enough for Coach to make my horrible day even WORSE! He divided teams by going around telling each kid that they were either a 1 or a 2. NATURALLY, Miranda was a 1 and I was a 2. Luckily Sophie was also a 2, so we were on the same team.

But that meant we were playing against Miranda, who was the STAR player. Is there ANYTHING that girl can't do?? Of course, Josh was on her team. OF COURSE! (At least Tyler and Matt were playing with Sophie and me.)

Me: WHY on EARTH are we doing this? I'm a fashion designer, NOT a volleyball player! We are going to get CRUSHED!

Sophie: I agree— the timing stinks! Just let Tyler or Matt go back and forth hitting it over.

Me: But I HAVE to serve eventually! You have to have arms of steel to serve that dumb ball. Miranda has strong arms because she has to carry around her ten pounds of makeup and hair spray!

Sophie: You're acting all crazy again, Catie. Calm down!

Me: Just pray that I can get this dumb ball over the net when I serve. I'm serious— PRAY!

   Then P.E. class got TOTALLY WEIRD. Even though Miranda had every reason on the planet to be happy, excited, and a show off on the court, she didn't spike the ball one single time.

NOT ONCE.

She would set the ball up and then let everyone else take turns hitting it over the net.

STRANGE. What was with her?

I couldn't help but stare. Was she sick? Had Emily finally come to her senses and told her to GET LOST? I couldn't say that I blamed her for THAT. . . . My mind kept wondering what was up. And I must have REALLY been out of it for a second—otherwise I would have SEEN IT COMING. **THAT IS, I WOULD HAVE SEEN JOSH SPIKE THE BALL IN MY DIRECTION!**

Sophie ducked quickly when Josh pounded the ball over the net. And standing behind her was LUCKY ME. **NOT.** **The ball SMACKED me right in the face.**

I went to the floor. I was almost positive that my nose was broken. It was even MORE embarrassing than the mustard disaster! Some of the kids gathered around and looked at me like some freak lab experiment.

Sophie rushed over and helped me stand up. So did Josh.
He was the LAST PERSON ON EARTH I wanted to talk to!
Of course he said he was sorry for spiking the ball like that.

BLAH, BLAH, BLAH!!!!!

The only good thing to come from being hit in the face was I got to go home early. Coach Calloway called Mom and acted like I was some third grader hurt on the playground. SHEESH!!!!!

By the time Mom arrived at school, my nose was TOTALLY SWOLLEN. It looked just like the nose on the Germ's Mr. Potato Head.

HIDEOUS!

WHO CARES ABOUT A DUMB DANCE NOW?!

I'm soooo ready to go to Arizona! Maybe the rez will accept one more kid . . . as in FOREVER!

MORE LATER!!!!!! GOTTA PACK!!!!!

We're finally headed for the airport.
YES!!!

After the VOLLEYBALL embarrassment, Mom actually felt sorry for me and said I could use her phone to text Sophie. I didn't have any time to waste!

Sophie: Sorry you had such a horrible day. And now you have to travel! Is your nose better?

Me: Thnx, Soph. It's better if you consider a nose the size of an avocado to be normal.

Sophie: Oh, stop it. Keep me posted on your trip, and I'll give you any updates from school and get your makeup work. I wish I could visit a rez. BORING here, so you're not missing anything. CU LATER, BFF!

We finally made it to Arizona and drove to Trinity Church, where we're staying for a few days. They have a large gym and showers, so it's kinda like camping but without the bug bites. ☺

The only thing that STINKS (and I do mean STINKS!) is the Germ has to sleep in a cot next to me. ☹☹☹ AT LEAST he had to leave Rosey at home. THANK YOU, JESUS!

Pastor Coleman, the group leader, came by and told us all about the Apache people. His church was really excited about us coming to help and had even collected clothing to pass out to kids who needed them.

Suddenly I felt like a TOTAL LOSER obsessing about that goofy dress at *Unique Boutique*. Mom had even been nice enough to pick it up before we left and hang it in my room.

Hopefully I can take it back when I get home. After all, I'm the LAST PERSON who needs it now! ☹

TIME TO HIT THE SACK!

I.

AM.

EXHAUSTED!!!!

WEDNESDAY, APRIL 7

Before we left for the rez this morning, Dad reminded us of **Matthew 28:19:** "Go, therefore, and make disciples of all nations, baptizing them in the name of the Father and of the Son and of the Holy Spirit."

After Dad read the passage in the Bible, I really understood why we were at the rez. I was even able to tolerate the Germ a little easier. But I wasn't sure how we were going to tell the Apache people about Jesus.

I'll admit that I was a little nervous about going to the reservation. What if they don't like us? What if they think the Germ and I are total WEIRDOS?

Of course, the Germ IS a weirdo, so one out of two isn't bad. ☺

WEIRDO

But when we finally arrived at the rez, things went better than I'd imagined. Mr. Coleman introduced Mom and Dad to the tribal elders, and they looked over the plans for the next few days. Then we FINALLY got to meet a bunch of the kids!

I was totally surprised to see everyone wearing T-shirts and jeans, just like the Germ and I. STRANGE. For some crazy reason, I thought I might see some cool Native American fashions, but NO SUCH LUCK. Dad reminded me that the Apache only wear fancy tribal clothes when they're going to a powwow or some other sacred ceremony.

DUH. ☹

Two of the girls on the rez were close to my age. Kai (whose name stands for "tall like a willow tree") and Eleni (whose name means "intelligence") like a lot of the same things that I do. We even like the same music!

But why don't I have a cool name like *Kai* or *Eleni*? I had absolutely no clue what *Catie* meant and made a mental note to ask Mom about it later. I wouldn't be surprised if it stands for "unpopular," or "girl who doesn't dance." I'm sure it's something lame like that.

Within a few hours, Mom and the other helpers had transformed the rez into an all-out VBS.

Welcome to
Spirit Ministries VBS!

SCHEDULE
10:00 Praise and Worship
11:00 Missions Around the World
12:00 LUNCH!!!
1:00 Lesson
2:00 Recreation/Crafts
3:00 Closing Song

Dad led the praise and worship, and Mom led the missions hour. The Germ and I hung out with all of the other kids.

Mom talked about how kids in many different parts of the world aren't even ALLOWED to learn about Jesus.

I couldn't believe it! There are even kids my age that RISK THEIR LIVES just so they can pray and read the Bible. THAT IS SOOO CRAZY!!

On another note, **LUNCH WAS DELICIOUS!**

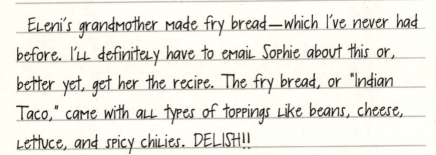

Eleni's grandmother made fry bread—which I've never had before. I'll definitely have to email Sophie about this or, better yet, get her the recipe. The fry bread, or "Indian Taco," came with all types of toppings like beans, cheese, lettuce, and spicy chilies. DELISH!!

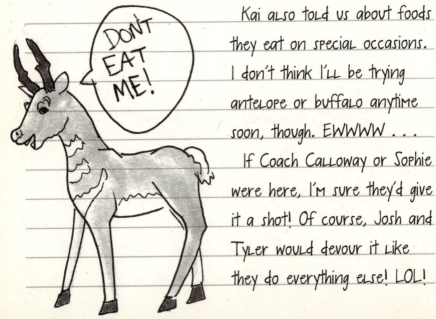

Kai also told us about foods they eat on special occasions. I don't think I'll be trying antelope or buffalo anytime soon, though. EWWWW . . .

If Coach Calloway or Sophie were here, I'm sure they'd give it a shot! Of course, Josh and Tyler would devour it like they do everything else! LOL!

Just thinking about them reminded me of all the embarrassing junk that had happened at school. ☹ I doubt if Kai or
Eleni ever has to worry about girls like Miranda Maroni!
   At least the swelling on my nose was almost gone. Life
on the rez was starting to look better and better. . . .

   Dad gave a message called "God as Our Creator" and
talked about **Genesis 1:26–27.** "Then God said, 'Let Us
make man in Our image, in Our likeness. They will rule the
fish of the sea, the birds of the sky, the livestock, all the
earth, and the creatures that crawl on the earth.'"
   Dad's lesson was pretty awesome, even if he is old school.
I could tell the people on the rez were really thinking
about his words. He reminded everyone that instead of wor-
shipping the sky, the rivers, or nature, we need to worship
the one who CREATED all of these things. YES!!!!

I also learned how important the land is to the Apache people. Eleni told me a really wild story about what happened to her tribe many years ago. She referred to it as the exodus of her people, and it sounded HORRIBLE. I couldn't believe that her ancestors were forced off land that was actually theirs to begin with. **HOW WRONG WAS THAT?**

It was interesting, though, that she called it an Exodus. . . . hmmmm . . .

NOTE TO SELF: Share the Bible with Eleni and Kai, and tell them the story about the Exodus in the Bible. Even though what happened to the Jews totally stunk, God watched over them—just like He watches over the Apache people too!

I told Kai that I could totally understand feeling like stuff wasn't fair (like Josh and Miranda—even though that isn't anything like what happened to her ancestors). However, we have to trust God's Word and hang on to His promises. It's easy to say but **WAY HARD TO DO!**

I COULD NOT BELIEVE WHAT ELENI AND KAI TOLD ME NEXT:

There's a girl on the rez named Tadi who acts JUST LIKE Miranda! She doesn't play volleyball, but she brags nonstop about all of her stuff. ☹ Eleni said she also says OUT LOUD that the boys think she's the prettiest girl on the rez— AND she wins almost every dance contest at the powwow.

Good grief!

The three of us decided that we REALLY need to pray for both Tadi and Miranda! Dad also reminded us that we need to pray for one another to be more patient as well.

UGH . . . why do Dads have to be right so much?

VBS was a blast with Eleni and Kai. I talked Mom into letting me take the lead and organize the first activity. I can't believe I'm admitting this, but I even allowed the Germ to be my assistant. Yes, that's what I said—he was my helper. **That fry bread must have fried my brain.**

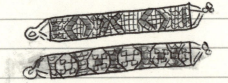

I decided our first craft would be a beaded bracelet with a cross. I'd brought all kinds of beads from my craft box at home and needed to put them to good use. From wooden beads to turquoise, I had it covered. The Germ carried around the craft box behind me, and each kid picked out the beads he or she wanted. By the end of the hour, the Germ and I had told everyone about Jesus and that the bracelet could be a reminder of His love. Eleni, Kai, and I decided to make bracelets that matched and promised to wear them everyday. IT WAS SO COOL! I even made Sophie one as a souvenir.

Of course, the Germ had to make one for him and Rosey as well. **That was pushing it.**

218

But after we'd made our bracelets, Kai totally surprised us. She ran next door to her house and brought over some REAL beaded Apache stuff! EVERYTHING WAS BEAUTIFUL! I'd never seen belts, moccasins, and leather pouches so pretty. Kai's mom had taught her how to do beading when she was younger because it's an important craft for her tribe. If only I could make bracelets like that! Maybe Kai could give me a quick lesson?

Kai's fancy stuff made my little VBS bracelet look a little plain.

Scratch that, it looked A LOT PLAIN. ☹

But Kai reminded me that our matching bracelets stood for something that was way more important: JESUS! ☺ ☺ ☺

At the end of the day, we did a closing song that was one of my favorites— "How Great Is Our God"!
Sophie and I always sing it at the top of our lungs at church. I could tell that most kids on the rez hadn't heard of it. But by Thursday, I'd make sure they did!! ☺

"How great is our God—sing with me. . . ."

TTYL . . .

We finally made it back to the church, and I am SO TIRED!! Even though things are going great at VBS, I'm trying NOT to do the following:

1. Obsess about what my friends are doing at home! (After all, I already know!)

2. Think about the big dance that I'm NOT even going to.

3. Be depressed about having to return my beautiful dress from Unique Boutique.

PRAY!
PRAY!
PRAY!

So Long,

Beautiful Dress!

THURSDAY, APRIL 8

I did not sleep last night . . . AT ALL!!!!!

I feel like a walking zombie, thanks to THE GERM. So now I'm WIDE AWAKE at 7 AM and writing in my diary! GRRRRRRRR . . .

WHY don't they make muzzles for brothers who SNORE LOUD ENOUGH TO WAKE THE DEAD?

I threw a pillow at his head TWICE and even threatened to duct tape his mouth shut. STILL NO LUCK. The Germ's snoring went from sounding like Darth Vader to sounding like a pig with hay fever.

I can't take IT *ANYMORE!*

I PRAYED FOR PATIENCE WITH THE GERM FOR THE 3,000TH TIME!

Where is Sophie when I need her? I decided to send her a message this morning and check out what's going on. Even though I'm not going to the dance. ☹ I'll get back in time to help her with her hair. ☹

222

Me: Hi from the rez! What R U doing?

Sophie: Just getting ready for school. ☹ Bio quiz in Finkleman's class. U can borrow my notes when U get back. What's up?

Me: Getting ready to go to VBS. It's actually pretty cool. What's the latest on the dance?

Sophie: Your guess is as good as mine! I did finally find a dress tho. Well, I borrowed one from a friend of Mom's. She has a daughter who's my size and said I could wear it. LOVE it plus saving a little $ $. ☺

Me: SWEET! I'm sure it will look amazing! Have u talked to Matt? He'll probably be so shy that he won't even dance. LOL.

Sophie: I know, right?! We're just friends, so it's no big deal. Haven't heard a single word about J and M. . . .

Me: Trying not 2 think about it. ☹ We should get home Saturday. Will B over ASAP! GTG. The rez is calling! C'YA

I think I'm starting to get a LITTLE homesick. I'm also still a LITTLE sad that Sophie's going to the dance and I'm not. Oh, and I'm SURE that Miranda is back home getting her nails done, picking out earrings, blah blah blah. She's probably bossing Emily around like an army sergeant!

As for Josh, I'm sure he's totally forgotten about flattening my nose with a volleyball!

Why am I even THINKING about THEM at a time like this?!

Even though it kills me to admit it, Josh has never given me any reason not to like him as a friend. UNLIKE Miranda, he's actually NICE—he even volunteers to lead prayer in our Bible class. Even people who aren't shy have a hard time leading prayers sometimes, but he does a great job. Maybe I'm being too hard on him?

But I'm NOT being too hard on Miranda! NO WAY.

Sometimes I have trouble understanding **WHY** God allows Miranda to be so rude, **WHY** I didn't get asked to the dance, and **WHY** I'm the one with the super annoying brother? Sometimes, I just don't get it!

Me: It's just NOT fair. Miranda is a total mean girl, but the cutest guy in class asks her to the dance. She makes fun of my fashions and even laughs when bad things happen to me. I'm tired of it.

Mom: First of all, you need to tell God about it, Catie. Remember in the Bible when King David lost his son? Or when Job had all of his problems? They both told God why they were angry. That's what we're supposed to do.

Me: Even if I DO tell God, how will that help with all this junk that is happening to me?

MOM: God knows what's best for you, even though it might not make sense at the time. Maybe He hasn't answered your prayers for a reason. Trust me on that. And more important, trust HIM.

Almost time for VBS. Gotta go wake up snoring Darth Vader. . . . **GRRRRR**

ooo CATIEooo

TODAY WAS AWESOME—even though I fell asleep four times!

When we got to the rez this morning, there were way more kids than the day before. **YES!** Word was starting to spread. ☺

After praise and worship, Mom taught a lesson about kids who live in Siberia, Russia. TALK ABOUT COLD!!! Missionary families travel to villages on dogsleds! Not only do they teach about Jesus, they also operate the only medical clinic for hundreds of miles. Some of the kids in Siberia only get to attend church a few times a year.

Being the fashion designer that I am, I couldn't help but wonder what kind of winter coats they wear in Siberia!

NOTE TO SELF:
Design a winter coat for missionaries!

The Germ went nuts when Mom talked about dogsleds. He went on and on and on with dumb facts about Siberian Huskies! IT FIGURES.

Maybe I can talk the Germ into going with Rosey to Siberia! Now THAT would be sweet! (Just kidding. ☺)

Dad's lesson was on God as our Savior. He explained to everyone the importance of John 3:16. Because Jesus died for our sins, we can become a new person. Kai and Eleni looked a little confused.

Kai: I don't get it. How can I become a new person when I'm twelve years old already?

Me: It's easy. Just ask Jesus to come into your heart.

Kai: Huh? What's the catch?

Me: There's no catch. ☺ After that, you're a new person and turn away from your old sinful life. Even though we still totally mess up, we're forgiven because Jesus went before us. Check out **Isaiah 43:1-2.** The Lord says, "I have called you by your name; you are Mine. I will be with you when you pass through the waters."

Kai: Wow. I had no idea. Can you show me a little more of the things He said?

Today's craft hour was HILARIOUS! The Germ would probably call it something else, but hilarious is the perfect word.

I should have known something was up when he came to the craft area with a bandanna on his head. . . .

My crazy brother had somehow talked Mom

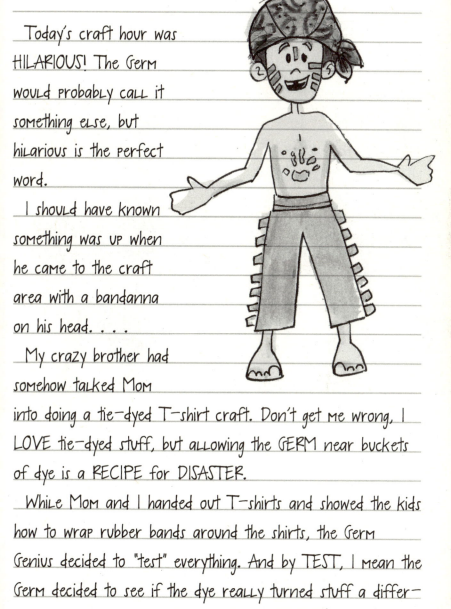

into doing a tie-dyed T-shirt craft. Don't get me wrong, I LOVE tie-dyed stuff, but allowing the GERM near buckets of dye is a RECIPE for DISASTER.

While Mom and I handed out T-shirts and showed the kids how to wrap rubber bands around the shirts, the Germ Genius decided to "test" everything. And by TEST, I mean the Germ decided to see if the dye really turned stuff a different color. And by STUFF, I mean his **HEAD!**

IT WAS PRICELESS!

It took me a few minutes to wrestle him to the ground, but when I finally pulled off the bandanna, I almost passed out from laughing!

HIS HEAD LOOKED LIKE A RAINBOW SNOW CONE!

All of the kids on the rez cracked up! The Germ ran inside and hung out with Dad the rest of the afternoon.

I cannot believe I'm saying this, but I actually felt sorry for Jeremy. Maybe it was because I remember how it felt when Miranda made fun of me. Or when I smiled at Josh with a hunk of broccoli between my teeth.

I talked Jeremy into standing beside me when we sang "How Great Is Our God" with the rest of the group. I also glanced over at Eleni and Kai. They now knew every word to the whole song!

YES!!!

I saw them practicing it this morning after reading their Bibles we'd given them. Now THAT was an answer to a prayer!

THANK YOU GOD!

FRIDAY, APRIL 9

I can't believe it. The time has FLOWN by SO fast.
Tomorrow is my last day on the rez. ☹

After hearing stories about missionaries on the other side
of the world, not to mention the people in my own country
who don't know about Jesus, that crazy school dance was
beginning to seem a little . . . well . . . **CRAZY.**

Maybe I overreacted a little about the whole Miranda and
Josh thing. . . . I was ready to forget all about it and help
Mom get ready.

Dad's last lesson was "God as Our Enabler." He reminded
us of **I CORINTHIANS 12:4-7:** "Now there are different
gifts, but the same Spirit. There are different ministries, but
the same Lord. And there are different activities, but the
same God activates each gift in each person."

I wasn't quite sure what Dad was trying to say and talked
with him about it at lunch.

Me: God may have given us all different gifts, but I have NO CLUE what mine is supposed to be. Not. A. Clue.

Dad: Sure you do. I can easily think of several: you're very creative, you're a great artist, and you have great fashion sense.

Me: You really think so? Thanks, Dad. But it's not like that MEANS anything. I want to serve God, but I really doubt I can do that with a sketch pencil and paper.

Dad: Maybe you should sit still and let God decide that. What's inside your heart is what matters, and it leads us to serve God in different ways. Just wait, you'll see in due time.

Sometimes I really don't like the words *in due time*. To me that feels like "it's never going to happen!" ☹

But I don't have time to think about that now. The rez kids and their tribal elders just announced they have a surprise for our family at lunch. *MORE LATER!*

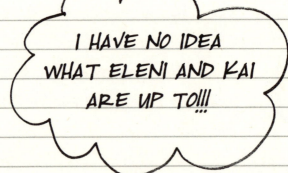

235

THIS WAS THE BEST DAY I'VE EVER HAD AT ANY VACATION BIBLE SCHOOL!

After the praise service, Mom and I got together the supplies for the perfect craft: picture frames.

For the last two days, Dad has been taking photos of everyone without telling them about Mom's frame surprise. After a little help from the Germ and me, each kid painted a wooden picture frame and decorated the sides with painted bottle caps. Kai and Eleni freaked when Dad gave them a picture he'd taken of the three of us. Kai spelled out **Jesus = Love** on her frame, and Eleni wrote **B.F.F.** on hers. I made one too and couldn't wait to put the picture of us in my room.

BUT THAT'S NOT THE HALF OF IT: The tribe decided that because it was our last day on the rez, they'd host a small POWWOW to celebrate everything they'd learned about Jesus. Can you say **AWESOME????**

Every single person on the rez wore colorful costumes. Eleni and Kai looked like princesses in their native leather-hide dresses. VERY FASHIONABLE. Eleni even wore a turkey feather in her hair. THEY LOOKED AMAZING. Their parents wore pants and shirts made out of buffalo hides, and beautiful beaded belts were tied around their waists.

BUT. THEN. IT. HAPPENED: Eleni and Kai invited us to JOIN THEM in the dance!

I COULD NOT BELIEVE IT!

Eleni tied a beautiful leather belt with feathers around my waist and also surprised me with a long turquoise necklace. Kai surprised me with two beaded bracelets that wrapped around my wrists. I'm sure that it took a LONG time to make them because the beads were so tiny. Kai actually GAVE them to me! ☺ She said it was to thank me for telling her about Jesus.

Maybe I was beginning to see one of my gifts from the Spirit. ☺ Maybe it was simply telling others about Jesus!

Eleni's dad gave my dad a small drum as a gift, and Kai's grandmother wrapped a beautiful woven shawl around Mom's shoulders.

One of the Apache boys even gave the Germ a headband with feathers and had braided a miniature one for Rosey.

Then all of us danced to the beat of Apache drums, held hands, and thanked God for His Son. **IT WAS THE BEST DANCE EVER.**

I couldn't wait to tell Sophie!

SATURDAY, APRIL 10

It stunk having to tell everyone good-bye, but we promised we'd be back. Maybe if we save our money and really try to cut corners, we can afford to stay longer next time and bring more supplies. To be perfectly honest, I don't need any new clothes, and I certainly don't have to have a new cell phone. That seems totally weird now.

While we waited at the airport, Dad was already hard at work on his laptop. Hopefully his new article, "A Powwow for Jesus" will draw enough interest so other families might visit the rez too. Mom was making notes on ways to make the mission trip even better if we come back next year.

Who knows, maybe I'll write an article for the school newspaper. **I'LL BE A FASHION DESIGNER AND A NEWS REPORTER!**

Of course, it's hard to even THINK about an article with the Germ sitting beside me on the plane. Even though he had on his headphones while watching a movie on Mom's laptop, EVERYONE could hear him giggling. It was so embarrassing . . . AND so annoying!

"Can you keep it down a little?" I asked. "Everyone on the plane doesn't want to hear what's funny in Finding Nemo. We've seen it already!"

But my brother totally ignored me and went back to laughing hysterically. I'll admit, though, he was watching the funniest part. Maybe I'll listen in for just a few minutes.

MORE LATER. . . . That crazy fish, Dory, cracks me up!

After we watched *Finding Nemo*, I fell sound asleep. The Germ finally woke me up when he punched me in the leg with his big foot. He SAID he'd been dreaming that he was fighting off a shark in his sleep. I wasn't sure if I believed him.

I was MORE than ready to go home and SLEEP IN MY OWN BED with the GERM NOWHERE AROUND!

MORE LATER . . . I HAVE SOME SLEEPING TO DO!!!! G'NIGHT!

SUNDAY, APRIL 11

I am still SO TIRED from the flight.

Maybe Mom will let me sleep in and not go to church today?

Zzzzzzzzzzzzzz . . .

244

Of course she said NO. "Sometimes being obedient to God's Word is hard, Catie, but you know it's the right thing to do," Mom reminded me.

She was right, but I was EXHAUSTED!

I even asked Dad if I could stay home—just this once. But his reply was the same as Mom's. "We need to be in fellowship with others, Catie. And I'm sure everyone will want to know all about the mission trip. I'm actually going to give the congregation a little overview of our trip."

I can't imagine getting in front of the entire church and TALKING!

Sure, I've been up front before, but it was a LONG time ago when I was seven. I had to play a shepherd in the Christmas play. Our youth director didn't have enough boys to play the part, and so Mom volunteered ME to do it. ☹ I DID have the most fashionable outfit of any shepherd though. ☺

I guess I'd better get to church and support Dad. I was also excited to see Sophie and catch up on everything at school. I can only imagine the homework I'll have to make up. ☹ Luckily Sophie promised to help me, especially with the math and science part.

I suddenly wondered what Kai and Eleni were doing back at the reservation. Maybe I'll write them a letter later. . . . GOTTA GO!! TTYL!!

Dad did a good job! He'd even created a short video to give everyone an idea of what happened on the trip. I wished he could have left out the part where my hair was totally a wreck. But I was glad to see he'd included the Germ with his rainbow hair! LOL! Everyone at church giggled a little. I could also tell they were impressed by the pictures of the powwow and liked the picture of me praying with Eleni and Kai.

Our pastor talked about the importance of spreading the gospel. He even challenged us to invite some of our friends to church. I couldn't imagine inviting Miranda. I felt terrible for feeling that way, but I couldn't help it. She'd probably say "Thanks, but NO THANKS" and laugh at me anyway.

I wondered if Miranda even knew about Jesus . . . because she sure doesn't act like it! Like when she brag brag brags about her Dad's big job or her Mom's new car. *Who does she think she is?* Even though my Dad bought a new SUV for my Mom last month, I didn't go to school and brag about it. That is so uncool. Instead, I said a prayer and thanked God for allowing our family to have a safe car to drive—especially when the roads are slick and Mom freaks out a little.

But I guess sometimes I don't act like I know Jesus either—like when I scream at the Germ and forget he's only in third grade. Or when I whine and get angry at Mom for not getting me a new phone . . .

NOTE TO SELF:
1. Pray about having the nerve to invite Miranda to church.
2. TRY to be nicer to the GERM.

MONDAY, APRIL 12

Even though I had a blast on the mission trip and missed my new friends, it was good to be back with my old friends. Matt asked a zillion questions about the Native Americans, and Sophie showed everyone the bracelet I gave her. Tyler didn't say much. Maybe he is still trying to fit in or something.

Of course, Miranda wasn't interested IN THE LEAST— not in anything that had to do with me.

ALL she talked about was THE DANCE. I had to overhear her tell EMILY about her appointment to have a mani-pedi, the perfect LIP GLOSS she'd found to match her dress, and the perfect photo to show her stylist of how she wanted her hair. ARE YOU SERIOUS?

I tried to remind myself of how I felt on the mission trip.

IT. IS. JUST.
A. DANCE.

Sure, I still wish that someone will ask me, but I know it isn't a big deal if it doesn't happen. Sophie tried to talk me into going again. I could meet up with her and Matt . . . but that would be sooo embarrassing.

Tyler didn't know if he was going either and said the dance wasn't a big deal to him. After all, he's new to our school and still doesn't know everyone. I overheard him tell Matt and Josh that he dared them to really dance and not just stand around like statues. LOL!

It would be sort of cool to see everyone dressed up. . . .

But I'm not sure I have the nerve to go by myself. I have a ton of science homework to make up. That could be my excuse for not going.

But when Sophie came over after school to help me with my makeup work, she said that was a lame excuse. "Come on, Catie," said my BFF. "Everyone's going to meet at the gym and just hang out together. The only one who's even calling it a date is Miranda, and who cares what she thinks! Besides, you already have that gorgeous Claire Hunter dress to wear."

Sophie did have a point. I hadn't even been able to look at that dress in my closet. I knew it would just make me sad all over again. I planned on giving it to Mom to take back to Unique Boutique.

To get my mind off of things, I decided to get out my sketchbook and draw something . . . ANYTHING. Maybe I'll design something for Kai and Eleni. Perhaps I'll design a new bag? Or a new skirt?

But I wasn't in the mood to draw anything. Maybe I'm not meant to be a fashion designer.

Maybe Miranda was right about me all along.

TUESDAY, APRIL 13

At least I had art today.

I hadn't seen Mrs. Gibson since I'd been back. I'm sure she was busy getting ready for the Middle School Art Show that was coming up on Monday. I was sooooo nervous and even begged Mrs. Gibson to give us a tiny hint of who the winner was. Her answer was "You'll just have to wait and see." Of course.

I was still hoping I could snap out of it and get in the mood to draw again.

What is **WRONG WITH ME?**

We were practicing mixing paint, and the only color I wanted to mix was gray. **Or black.** I wasn't feeling very colorful today. Mrs. Gibson could tell that something was wrong.

"Are you feeling okay, Catie?" she asked. "I can't wait to hear about your mission trip. I'm sure you saw lots of things that will inspire your new fashion designs."

"Maybe," I said. "Right now, I'm just not feeling it."

Then Mrs. Gibson did the weirdest thing. She wrote a note to me and placed it on my desk:

Deuteronomy 31:6

Mrs. Gibson knew me so well!

Then she walked past me to help Sophie mix the right amount of yellow and red to make her favorite color.

At the end of class, I stopped by Mrs. Gibson's desk. "Thanks for the Bible verse," I said. "I'll look it up as soon as I get home. Oh, and you're right about the dance thing. Sophie's trying to talk me into going with her, but I'm still not sure I want to."

Not only did Mrs. Gibson always know what to do, but she also knew just what to say. "I remember going to a few dances when I was in school," she said. "Many times I'd just go with a group of friends, and we had so much fun. I didn't get nervous or worry about saying something wrong. I was with friends who liked me just the way I was."

Mrs. Gibson had a point. I noticed that Sophie was waiting on me in the hallway.

"I'll think about it, Mrs. Gibson," I said. "You're the best." I even reached over and gave her a hug. I didn't care who saw me.

But after Sophie and I got to P.E. class, we saw the STRANGEST THING: Miranda came in late, and we could tell she'd been crying.

HUH?

I'm sure it was over something ridiculous. She was probably upset that she couldn't find the perfect nail polish for the big dance. Or maybe she was stressed that she couldn't take a limo to the dance!

UGH.

It was hard to feel sorry for Miranda when she never feels sorry for ANYONE.

Sophie noticed that Miranda went to the bathroom several times too. Usually Emily went right after her.

What on earth was going on?

I asked Tyler if he had any idea what was up with Miranda, but he was clueless. In fact, Tyler acted a little strange when I brought up the whole dance thing.

Odd . . .

I was so ready to go home and forget about school . . . AND THE DANCE. Forget about Miranda, about Emily, about Tyler, about **EVERYONE.**

Well, everyone but Sophie . . . and Mrs. Gibson. I pulled out her note and looked up the verse:

Deuteronomy 31:6: "Be strong and courageous; don't be terrified or afraid of them. For it is the Lord your God who goes with you; He will not leave you or forsake you."

Just reading that verse made me feel so much better. I still wasn't sure about the dance, but I knew I should pray about it. For some reason, I even felt like sketching a few new designs.

YES! CATIE CONRAD, THE FASHION DIVA, WAS BACK IN ACTION!

WEDNESDAY, APRIL 14

WEIRD WEDNESDAY!!!!!

As soon as I walked thru the front door at school, Sophie pulled me by the arm into the bathroom.

Sophie: You are NOT going to BELIEVE what I'm about to tell you!

Me: Huh? What's going on? Tell me already!

Sophie: Okay, so get this— MIRANDA IS NOT GOING TO THE DANCE! Emily told Tyler, and Tyler told Matt, and Matt told me. Can you BELIEVE it?

Me: WHY? Did Josh change his mind?

Sophie: WHO KNOWS? He didn't tell me anything else. Hopefully by the end of the day, we'll get all the details.

Me: Maybe everyone in school is finally figuring out the REAL Miranda and the REAL Emily. Maybe everyone is starting to see just how RUDE they really are!

BUT. THEN. IT. HAPPENED.

Emily came out of one of the stalls in the bathroom. **I. WAS. SPEECHLESS.** I had NO IDEA that she'd been in there the whole time.

"Oh, uh, hi, Emily . . ." Sophie said. "We're really sorry—"

Emily gave us the meanest look ever and said NOTHING. She simply stormed out of the bathroom and marched down the hall. I bet she was looking for Miranda.

We were DOOMED. I could only imagine what Miranda would say to Sophie and me once we got to class.

But I still couldn't help but wonder why she wasn't going to the dance. **WHAT WAS GOING ON???**

This could be my big chance to go with Josh, right?

Why wasn't Miranda going? WEIRD. Maybe she was dumping Josh and going with someone else? That sounded like something she'd do.

But when we got to our first period class, Miranda wasn't there. The tardy bell rang, and she never showed up. Miranda was absent the entire day.

DOUBLE WEIRD.

And Josh was in a bad mood. I kept thinking MAYBE he'd get the nerve to ask me to the dance.

But he didn't. ☹

He only hung out with Tyler the entire day and was totally hush-hush about the dance. Of course, I didn't have the nerve to ask him what was going on. Neither did Sophie.

Now the only two of my friends who were going to the dance were Sophie and Matt! NOT Miranda, NOT Josh . . . and NOT ME!!!

THIS WAS THE CRAZIEST DAY EVER.

It got even crazier when we got to Sophie's house after school. I'd gone over to see her dress and help pick out the perfect jewelry and shoes. But Sophie got a text as soon as we got thru the door.

It was from EMILY!!!!!!!!!
HUH? Why would Emily message my best friend?

I was sure it was to chew us out for talking about her and Miranda in the bathroom this morning. But I was totally wrong. Get this—Emily asked us to PRAY for Miranda.
Whoa. What is happening???

Miranda isn't going to the dance because her dad LOST HIS JOB. Her parents have been fighting a lot for the last few weeks, and Miranda is REALLY UPSET. That's why she didn't come to school today. She's taken both dresses back, told Josh she can't go to the dance, and is too embarrassed to tell anyone. Except Emily.
WOW. I had no idea.

So Sophie and I prayed for Miranda. Yes, that's what I said—I PRAYED FOR THE MEANEST GIRL IN SCHOOL. I'm not sure why I did it, but I did it anyway. I couldn't help but think about Tadi—Eleni and Kai's friend on the rez. Maybe she had problems like Miranda.

THIS WAS THE WEIRDEST DAY
IN THE HISTORY OF WEIRDEST DAYS.

⑤ Prayer List

1. Miranda (I can't believe
   I just wrote that)
2. Mrs. Gibson (I'm so
   thankful she's my teacher!)

THURSDAY APRIL 15

Miranda was at school today.

EVERYONE noticed that she wasn't acting like the typical Miranda Maroni. She never said a word about the dance, and she never bragged about her stuff. She just hung out with Emily and kept to herself.

Even though I should be happy that Miranda wasn't being her typical rude self or bragging about her zillion outfits, I wasn't.

I felt sorry for her. I have NO IDEA why, but I did. Maybe it was because I thought about how I'd feel if my dad lost his job. Or if my parents argued all the time. That would STINK big time. Even worse than the Germ and Rosey!

Everyone else, including Principal Martin and the teachers, were getting excited about the dance. We couldn't even go to the gym for P.E.

because the decorations were TOP SECRET.

At least we got out of having to run laps. YES!!!

When I got home from school, I was still thinking about Miranda. Mom had laid down the law—I HAD to clean my room. I still hadn't totally unpacked from the mission trip, and clothes were lying all over the place.

As I slowly started picking everything up and putting my nice things on hangers, I noticed the Claire Hunter dress hanging in my closet. It was still the MOST GORGEOUS dress I'd ever seen. I hadn't asked Mom to take it back to Unique Boutique yet. I was still thinking about wearing it to the dance . . . by myself.

But after hearing the news about Miranda, I sorta knew what I needed to do. I told Sophie about it, and she totally agreed. Now if I could just get Mom and Dad to go along with it. As soon as Mom got home from work, I cornered her and Dad.

Me: Hey, uh, I need to talk with you two about something. Even though I'm not going to the dance, may I keep the turquoise dress from *Unique Boutique*?

Dad: What? Catie, that dress was expensive!

Mom: You even put your allowance money in on that dress. If you're not going to the dance, why not return it and get your money back?

Me: Well . . . to be honest . . . I'd like to give it to Miranda. Her dad lost his job, and she had to take back her dress. Now she's too embarrassed to go to the dance.

Mom: Wow. You've sure changed your attitude. That's really nice of you, Catherine. Do you remember when your friends on the rez told you the meaning of their names?

Did you know that I chose your name because it means "pure at heart"? I think you're proving that "Catherine" fits you perfectly.

Me: Thanks, Mom. But I don't want her to know the dress is from me. It might embarrass her more. It's okay if she doesn't know.

Dad: I'm so impressed with you, sweetie. I think I know some-one who's growing up. See how God works everything out?

Mom: I only have one question—how are you going to get that dress to Miranda without her knowing it's from you?

Me: Sophie and I have a plan. We are pros when it comes to

Operation: SPRING DANCE!

FRIDAY, APRIL 16

Once again, I could not sleep because of the Germ. Even though we'd been home for six days, his snoring was just as bad as it had been at the rez. At least he was in his own room now. BUT. I. STILL. HEARD. HIM.

Me: Hey, over there! You're snorting in your sleep like one of those weird animals on Animal Planet! Give it a rest!

Germ: Well, it doesn't bother Rosey, so it shouldn't bother you!

Me: Okay, so you're comparing me to a SKUNK? You have GOT to be KIDDING ME!

I couldn't wait to get to school and see Sophie. We were also eager to see Miranda and Emily . . . just to see what would happen next.

Get this. Emily told Josh, Josh told Tyler, and Tyler told me: Miranda was now going to the dance.
IMAGINE THAT!!! ☺
Miranda never mentioned why suddenly the dance was back on, but that was okay. Sophie and I knew the reason, and that was enough.

Then something SUPER SURPRISING happened. At the end of the day, while I was putting my books back into my locker, Tyler came up and started talking to me.
WEIRD.
WEIRD.
WEIRD.

Tyler: Uh, hi Catie. I haven't had time to ask you about your trip. Was it cool out there?

Me: Hey Tyler. Yeah, uh, it was fun.

Tyler: I tried to text you before your mission trip, but it didn't go thru or something.

Me: Oh, well, my phone doesn't text, so . . . what were you going to say? I know it's old news, but—

Tyler: No, uh . . . I . . . Well, I . . . thought I'd see if you're going to the dance tonight?

Me: I'm not sure about the dance. I don't actually have a dress.

Tyler: Oh . . . okay . . . Well, if you change your mind . . . maybe we could meet at the gym or something? I'm going with Matt.

Me: HMMM . . . okay . . . maybe—sure, I'll go. Sophie and I will meet you guys there. But remember, we're just friends—right?

Tyler: Duh. See ya tonight!

OH. MY. GOSH!!!!!!

I flew home and called Sophie. I didn't have time to just message her on the computer. I needed to talk to her ASAP!

EXCITED Me: Sophie, YOU MUST COME OVER . . . LIKE, RIGHT NOW!!!! I am GOING TO THE DANCE!!!!!

Sophie: I ALREADY HEARD!
Tyler texted Matt, and Matt told me. THIS IS GREAT NEWS. There's only one small problem —WHAT ON EARTH ARE YOU GOING TO WEAR?

Me: DUH! Why do you think I need you to come over? Oh, and I know I might sound bonkers, but maybe you should text Emily and ask if she wants to meet us there too? Maybe she felt the same way as I did about going to the dance.

Sophie: GREAT IDEA! It's worth a shot, but I'm not holding my breath. I'll text her on the way to your house. Be over in FIVE minutes!

Sophie flew through the door, and Mom wanted to know what all the drama was about. When I told her about Tyler talking to me at my locker, she was glad I had decided to say yes.

She said: "I'm sure you have something in your closet to wear. After all, you are my little fashion designer."

THAT'S WHEN I REMEMBERED MY TRÈS CHIC DRESS!!!! It wasn't perfect, but I'd finished hemming it before I left for the mission trip.

YES! YES!! YES!!!

I hurried into my room and opened my closet. Only the WORST THING HAPPENED: I. COULDN'T. FIND. THE. DRESS.

IT
WAS
GONE. ☹ ☹ ☹

Maybe it had fallen off the hanger? I looked in the floor of my closet, under my bed, and in my pile of dirty clothes. But it was nowhere to be found.

There was only one explanation: that crazy skunk had stolen my dress! I KNEW that stink bomb Rosey was nothing but trouble! This made me 100 percent sure!

  I marched into the Germ's room and started looking everywhere: under his bed, in his closet, and even in Rosey's
goofy little pet house. But I didn't even find a single sequin.

Upset Me: *WHERE did you put my dress? I know you or*
Rosey have it!

Annoying Germ: I don't have your dumb dress! And neither does Rosey! Why would she want your goofy dress? Duh! She has FUR—AND she happens to have excellent taste!

ACK!!! How does a dress just DISAPPEAR? Where did I put it?? I was totally freaking out. I had FINALLY decided to go to the dance, and now I would have to wear pajamas.

Thankfully, Sophie is great under pressure. She came up with a plan: get out my sewing machine and create a Catie Conrad Original dress!

Mom agreed with her.

WERE THEY INSANE??? Who could sew at a time like this?

Then Mom said to use that vintage dress I'd bought at Goodwill and finish the makeover I'd been working on.

With Mom and Sophie's help, I started cutting and sewing. I was sooo glad to have my fast new sewing machine for the job! Mom ironed, and Sophie handed me the sequins.

Sophie kept reminding me of **Philippians 4:13:** "I am able to do all things through Him who strengthens me."

Then she had to rush home and get ready herself! I don't know what on earth I'd do without my BFF.

More Later. . .
IF I SURVIVE!!!!

SATURDAY, APRIL 17

THE DANCE WAS AWESOME!!!!

Soooooo here's what happened:

Matt and Tyler waited outside of the gym for Sophie and me.

Sophie looked gorgeous in her dress. Coral was definitely her color. And believe it or not, I had JUST ENOUGH time to finish my C.C.O. dress!

I had to take a needle and thread in the car with me, and I sewed the last sequin on the bottom of the skirt just as Mom pulled into the parking lot to drop me off. WHEW!

The black sequins really gave it a little sparkle, even though I had had to chase Rosey down to get the last few. She'd run through the house acting crazy and slobbering all over the sequin packet. By the time the Germ caught up with her, she sparkled more than my dress.

I wore Kai's beaded bracelets on each wrist, and they were the PERFECT accessory!

I was sure that Miranda would laugh me off the face of the planet when she saw my homemade dress.

But she didn't.

And I didn't care if she did.

Anyway, she was too wrapped up in Josh to even notice. TYPICAL MIRANDA. But I'll admit it: my turquoise dress looked beautiful on her.

Catie: Hi, Miranda! Your dress is awesome.

Miranda: Oh, thanks, Catie. I love it myself! Turquoise IS my color isn't it? I just HAD to have it when I saw it in the window! Luckily the store had it in just my size!

Catie: HUH? Oh . . . uh . . . well, you look very nice. See ya 'round.

I couldn't believe it! Miranda LIED! How DARE she act like that! UGH. I SO wanted to call her out on it.
But I didn't. I asked myself how Jesus would act about the whole thing, and I already knew the answer: He wouldn't say anything. He'd pray for her, so that's what I did.

BUT IT WAS SO HARD.

I tried to forget about it and just have fun hanging out with Matt, Sophie, and Tyler. Even Josh was nice enough to walk over and tell me that he liked my dress!

Unfortunately, he knew I'd made it myself. Sophie was so proud of it that she'd told Matt, Matt had told Tyler, and Tyler had told Josh.

SHEESH!!!

But I tried to remember what Dad had said on the rez—that I shouldn't be ashamed of my gifts, like sewing and drawing. After all, God gave them to me!

I even tried to be happy for Miranda when she was crowned Princess of the Spring Dance. OF COURSE SHE WAS—she was MIRANDA MARONI, after all: the most popular girl in middle school.

So that's what happened, and now I GOTTA GO TO SLEEP! Dressing up and going to a dance is EXHAUSTING!

TTYL!

SUNDAY, APRIL 18

Even though I'd had fun at the dance, I was glad it was over. It was all enough to drive a girl bonkers!

When I got to church, Josh, Tyler, and Sophie looked like they were still tired too. Josh even admitted that he wished he'd hung out with us at the dance. I wondered if that meant that he wished he'd asked me to go, but I tried not to think about it. He said that all Miranda wanted to do was talk about her dress, her hair, her shoes, and on and on and on.

Sophie and I couldn't help but look at each other and smile. We knew the real story and the real Miranda.

Before we went home, everyone agreed that next year, we ALL were gonna go as FRIENDS and not worry about getting asked OR asking someone to the dance. THANK GOODNESS. That would make things SOOOO much easier!

After church I decided to write Eleni and Kai a letter and send them a pic of me wearing the bracelets at the dance. I also decided to send each of them a fashion accessory that I'd made myself. Since I'd cleaned my room and could actually see my sewing machine, I planned on spending

the rest of the day designing each of them a belt. Maybe they could wear them at their next powwow!
  LOTS OF DESIGNING TO DO! ☺ ☺ ☺

Prayer List:
1. Thank God for giving me so many great friends who understand me.
2. Thank Him for allowing everyone to have such a great time at the dance!!

MONDAY, APRIL 19

TODAY WAS THE DAY: THE MIDDLE SCHOOL ART SHOW.

But all that everyone wanted to talk about was the dance.

Some of us had printed off pics and put them up in our lockers. Just looking at the pics of me and my friends acting silly caused me to count my blessings. I SO overreacted about things.

I wish Emily had shown up at the dance, but she didn't. Maybe we'll talk her into it when the next dance rolls around. After all, it does take a little nerve.

Today she was too wrapped up in listening to Miranda tell EVERYONE about the dance and her being crowned Princess. Miranda had even worn the tiara to school. UGH. Some things never change.

But the only thing I could think of was my très chic dress drawing. What if the judges thought it STUNK? I'd worked so hard on it, but everyone has different tastes when it comes to fashion. Just ask Miranda. ☹

After lunch, everyone in school had to gather in the gym to attend the art show. I WAS SOOO NERVOUS!

Sophie seemed just as excited as me. She'd entered the photography category and turned in a collage of different dessert pictures. It looked good enough to eat.

But when I walked through the gym door, I instantly noticed the most AWESOME, AMAZING, INCREDIBLE THING EVER:

IT WAS MY REAL
TRÈS CHIC DRESS . . .
ON A MANNEQUIN!!!
HUH? HOW DID IT GET THERE??

And that's not the only thing:
MY DRESS WON BEST
IN SHOW!!!!!

I WAS SO EXCITED!!
. . . and SO CONFUSED.

I also noticed that Mrs. Gibson and Sophie were smiling from ear to ear.

"Congratulations, Catie Conrad," said Mrs. Gibson, hugging me. "I knew you could do it. It's a masterpiece. Van Gogh would be proud."

"But how did you get my dress? How?" I was happy yet still didn't understand.

But Sophie did. "Remember how I promised you guys that I'd feed Rosey while you were on the mission trip? I sorta sneaked into your closet and turned in your dress to Mrs. Gibson. I knew it could win, and I was right!"

I couldn't help but cry. I had the most awesome best friend in the universe.

I asked Mrs. Gibson to take a pic of me and Sophie with my award. I couldn't wait to put it up in my locker tomorrow.

When I got home, I gave Mom the $25 prize money to send to the mission in Arizona. I knew that Eleni's and Kai's families could use the money.

I also decided to get back to work on some new dress sketches. Sophie had talked me into creating a dress for her too. Since we were brave enough to wear my shirt designs to school, we decided to wear our C.C.O. dresses next!

So there you have it. **THE BEST DAY OF MY LIFE!!!** Miranda still drives me crazy, but I won't stop praying for her . . . and for Emily.

I think I'll invite them to church next week.

Oh, and I also apologized to Jeremy . . . and to Rosey. My brother actually seemed excited that I'd won the art show. Even that crazy skunk seemed happy. ☺

I can't believe I've used up every single page in this crazy diary.

WEIRD!

Luckily, Dad bought two for the price of one and then went back for extras.

After all, a fashion diva needs LOTS of paper. ☺

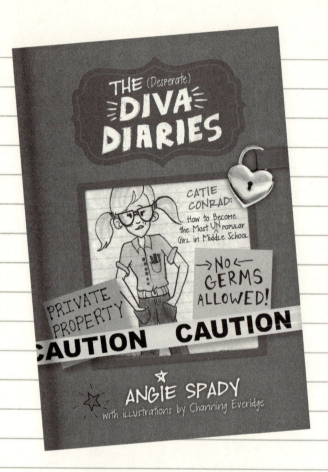

COMING SOON!

Since Dad gave me more diaries to fill up,

I'd better get started now. . . .

Here's a sneak peek at my next adventures!

SATURDAY, JANUARY 17

I CANNOT believe that I've already filled up an entire diary and I'm starting on the second!
WEIRD.

If anyone had ever told me (especially DAD) that I'd write my most PRIVATE secrets in a crazy diary, I'd think that:
A. They'd totally lost it.
B. Their elevator didn't go all the way to the top.
C. They must have me mixed up with some kind of brainiac kid.
D. All of the above.

But Dad was right. This diary thing is kinda cool—ESPECIALLY when I've had a horrible day at school . . . *LIKE TODAY.*
Or when I need to come home, forget about Miranda Maroni, and just design stuff in my sketchbook . . .
LIKE TODAY.

It all started in P.E. . . .

Did I mention that I do NOT like P.E. class? Well I don't, and neither does my best friend, Sophie. Maybe it's because Coach Calloway treats us like we're in the army. One minute he's saying "drop and do me 25 push ups!" and the next he's yelling, "the next kid who complains is going to do 1,000 laps around the gym!" Well, maybe he didn't say 1,000 laps, but it was something like that. I wouldn't be surprised if he blows that whistle one of these days and makes us scrub the toilets with a toothbrush.

But today it wasn't Coach Calloway that put me in a bad mood—it was Miranda.

OF COURSE.

Miranda Maroni is the one girl in sixth grade who knows exactly how to get on my LAST NERVE. ☹ Whether it's rolling her eyes when I wear one of my fashions to school, or her NONSTOP bragging about the "the latest accessory to die for," she drives me INSANE!

Miranda may not have been driving me crazy today, but she was being a total pain to Sophie. ☹

I guess I should mention that Sophie is captain of the middle school academic team. And if you ask me, the Clairemont Crusaders are LUCKY to have her.

GO CRUSADERS!

She not only scores more points than anyone else, she's also the smartest and most organized girl I know. The exact OPPOSITE of me. ☹ I can't remember the dates of boring old wars (why do we need to know that kind of stuff anyway?), and I can barely remember to study for those crazy algebra quizzes. (Who on earth needs to know the value of X+Y?!)

But Sophie never forgets a single thing. She even messages me at home to remind me of our homework assignments. THANK YOU, SOPHIE!

But after Coach Calloway made us sprint up and down the gym today (I almost passed out twice), Sophie decided to get out her study questions and prepare for the next academic meet.

Naturally, since I'm her BFF, I offered to quiz her until the bell rang. Sophie recited names of classical music composers one minute, and the next she rattled off science definitions word for word! I don't know how that girl does it.

AND for some reason that makes NO SENSE to me, Miranda decided to be her typical bully self. "Why are you wasting your time on that stupid academic team, Sophie?" she asked. "Talk about BOR-ING! Why don't you forget about that junk and try out for the volleyball team—a group that actually KNOWS how to WIN!"

.UGH.

Yeah, she actually said that. Of course I shouldn't be surprised. She's Miranda Maroni: the RUDEST girl in class. ☹

You could have heard a pin drop in the gym after Miranda blurted out her two cents. I was almost sure that my mouth dropped open. Everyone in class waited to see what Sophie would say back to her.

"Whatever, Miranda," Sophie said. "Thanks, but I'll stick with the academic team. Good luck on your volleyball match against the Lions, though."

HUH?? I couldn't believe it. Sophie was actually NICE to her.

I don't know if I could have acted like Sophie. I'd want to say "Thanks but NO THANKS, Miranda! Why would I want to be on a volleyball team with YOU? I'm WAY smarter than you'll ever be!"

But I'd only say that in my head. Even though I sometimes totally stink at it, I try to remind myself of **Psalm 34:13:** "Keep your tongue from evil and your lips from telling lies."

So yeah, I try to keep my mouth shut. But it's SO HARD with M.M.!!!

  I practically pray for her every week since she drives me bonkers on a daily basis. Of course, I pray for myself, too, since I need a double dose of patience with her. Scratch that—TRIPLE DOSE!

  Sophie and I were never so glad to leave P.E. class today. Once again, Miranda and Coach Calloway had ruined a perfectly good morning. . . .

I could hardly wait to get home and vent about it in my diary. At least I can write down my feelings and talk to God about it. Of course, I can also get my mind off things by drawing in my sketchbook. ☺

After all, the world's next

FASHION DESIGNER TO THE ★ ★ ★

has to practice, practice, practice!

GTG!
There're some
GORGEOUS dress
designs in my
future!!!!

← Rhine Stones!

Purple →
leather!

NEW
FALL RUNWAY
COLLECTION!

BASH is back!

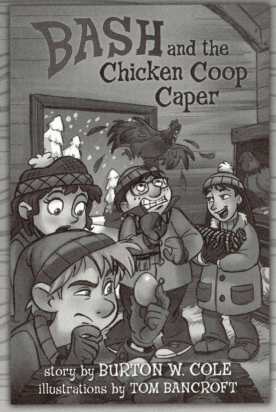

Humor ensues with the second book in a popular, new series in boys fiction from Burton W. Cole.

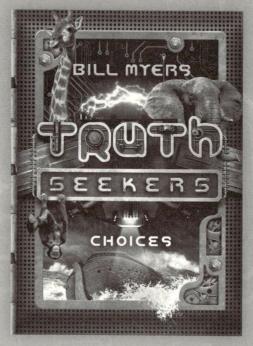